A Doctor Called Caroline

A cool, self-contained girl, tall and slight, with a reputation for brilliance: this was Caroline Milne, of the department of child health at the Central London Hospital.

Since her student days she'd planned to become a family doctor at her home in Stonebridge – so what was she doing falling in love with Daniel Harcourt, registrar to the professor, with his career firmly based in London?

At home, everyone seemed to be making demands on her. Jeremy wanted to marry her and, since her mother's death, Caroline's father depended on her. And then there was Sarah, the small patient whose parents were divorced and who lived with her mother in a caravan outside the town. She needed Caroline as much as any of them.

The problems and dramas of a busy teaching hospital, a world which Elizabeth Harrison knows well, makes a gripping background to this touching story of two hard-working young doctors whose love has to take second place to the demands of the hospital.

ELIZABETH HARRISON

A Doctor Called Caroline

HURST & BLACKETT

Hurst & Blackett Ltd
3 Fitzroy Square, London WIP 6JD

An imprint of the Hutchinson Publishing Group

London Melbourne Sydney Auckland
Wellington Johannesburg and agencies
throughout the world

First published 1979
© Elizabeth Harrison 1979

Set in Intertype Baskerville

Printed in Great Britain by The Anchor Press Ltd
and bound by Wm Brendon & Son Ltd
both of Tiptree, Essex

British Library Cataloguing in Publication Data

Harrison, Elizabeth
A doctor called Caroline.
I. Title
823'.9' 1F   PR6015.A648D/

ISBN 0 09138900 3

Contents

I

The New Registrar

In the department of child health at the Central London Hospital there were two main topics of conversation. First, the new registrar from Mortimer's, Daniel Harcourt, appointed over the heads of Central candidates who considered they had a prior – not to mention God-given – right to the post, and, second, Caroline Milne's pigheaded obstinacy.

'She'll be thrown away in general practice,' someone mourned.

'She doesn't seem to think so.'

There was a general groan.

'We're all aware of that.' Andrew Marshall, the department's senior registrar, was unusually acid.

Caroline was slim and dark, with the sort of quiet good looks, it was agreed, that grew on you – not sensational, but satisfying – and from student days she had firmly announced that she was qualifying for the purpose of joining her mother in general practice in Stonebridge, the country town where she had been brought up.

'Shocking waste,' someone said, a comment her friends had been making for years.

On the way down to the car park after the ward round Dr Walter Berkeley, the assistant director of the department, said it to Caroline herself. 'And why, for God's sake? Could you just give me one sound reason why you propose to throw a reasonably promising career down the drain like this?'

Caroline regarded him unhappily. 'But you know I've always planned – '

'That was when your mother was alive.'

Caroline flinched.

'I'm sorry to be brutal, but – well, it's no longer the same, is it? Any notion you had that you'd take some of the load off her shoulders – those days are gone. You surely aren't suggesting that you owe your mother's former practice the same loyalty?'

'In a way, I think I do.'

Dr Berkeley gave a short, irritated bark of annoyance. 'I wash my hands,' he said, entering his car and slamming the door.

Caroline walked back into the hospital. For as long as she could remember, almost, this was how her life had been mapped out for her. And with her mother's unexpected death, barely six months back, from a heart attack, it had seemed more certain, rather than less, that at the end of her two years as registrar to Dr Berkeley, she would return to Stonebridge and what had always been the Armstrong, Evans and Milne practice. At the Central, though, she was well aware they thought her decision dotty. Perhaps the unwelcome arrival of this new registrar from Mortimer's would at least give their thoughts a new slant.

There'd been speculation about Daniel Harcourt, and a number of unfriendly eyes were going to be focused on him as he trod the wards. Mortimer's, straggling down the northern slopes of the city towards Kilburn, acres of red brick erected in Victorian days, was staffed – according to Central gossip – by unpredictable eccentrics. Five years ago, they'd been forced to accept Sir Graham Williamson as Professor of Child Health – he was, they had to admit, next door to genius. And, typical of genius, they pointed out, he was on many counts nutty as a fruit cake, and inhabited a world of his own. But now came this second interloper from the same impossible place, who might prove to be the first of a flood from Mortimer's submerging the Central talent. The post of registrar to the professor was coveted, in any case, and a great many had been disappointed not to land it. They'd expect Daniel Harcourt to demonstrate within a day or two – if not an hour or two – that he deserved the post.

Andrew Marshall maintained that he did. Daniel Harcourt was outstandingly able, he said, and would be an asset to the department. Meeting Caroline on her way in, he invited her to join him for a meal that evening at his flat, for the purpose of briefing Daniel. 'That should take your mind off your own problems,' he added.

Caroline was nearing the end of her patience. 'I don't have problems,' she asserted wildly. 'I know what I'm doing. I've always known. It's everyone else who insists on turning my future into a problem.'

'Have it your own way,' Andrew said agreeably. 'We'll expect you around eight.' Square and stolid, he was seldom ruffled.

Caroline was held up in the ward, so, rather than keep the Marshalls waiting, she went straight across to their flat in St Anne's Square, round the corner from the hospital, without bothering to change. They were old friends, and they'd accept her in her old denim skirt and routine cheesecloth shirt, she knew. When she arrived in Andrew's cluttered sitting room, it was to find Daniel Harcourt already there. An untidy, rumpled-looking figure, long and gangling, with a mop of dark hair, he was extended – apparently thoroughly relaxed – in one of Andrew's ancient but comfortable armchairs, a tankard of beer on the floor beside him. He scrambled untidily and leggily to his feet, dropping several pieces of paper and his fountain pen, and shook hands. His eyes, that held a glint

9

of humour and yet something of tenderness too – at the Central they were to discover that children always trusted Daniel, would allow him to do the most amazing things to them, however painful – unexpectedly pierced Caroline to the heart. No one had ever looked at her like that.

Whatever his eyes might tell her, though, his voice merely stated politely and unemotionally that yes, they had met, he believed, when Sir Graham had taken him round the ward.

'That's right,' Caroline agreed, wondering why he had not had this extraordinary effect on her then – or, alternatively, why he should have it now. Accepting a glass of Cinzano bianco from Andrew, she willed the sensation to go away.

'Cinzano, with ice and lemon, is Caroline's drink,' Andrew said informatively, making conversation.

'I'll remember that,' Daniel said.

Caroline's heart turned over. He would? Did he mean it? Was he going to be taking her out, buying her drinks? She collapsed into the chair Andrew had drawn up for her, and sipped the drink with a carefully blank expression. This could not be happening. She had not, in a second or two, fallen helplessly in love. Had she?

She glanced cautiously across the coffee table, strewn with roneoed departmental lists and timetables, Andrew's stethoscope, his diary, his notebook, and several weeks *BMJ*s and *Lancet*s, and told herself she'd see a perfectly ordinary young man in a suit that needed pressing, a young man who was going to be a colleague, no more, for the next few months. No one special at all.

The dark eyes that had stabbed her two minutes earlier produced exactly the same effect when she encountered them again. Hastily, she began talking too fast about Sir Graham Williamson's views on the latest treatment for acute myeloid leukaemia.

As she gabbled, though she didn't suspect it, Daniel Harcourt was asking himself very much the same questions. This cool, self-contained girl in her striped cotton shirt, tall and slight, with her reputation for brilliance, surely could not possibly, in two seconds flat, have overturned his life? He had enough on his plate. With his new job and his new hospital, he needed a love affair about as much as he needed a hole in the head. He was damned if he was going to complicate his life at this juncture. No way. He too began talking rather fast about Sir Graham's views.

Over the washing up that night Andrew commented to his wife. 'I'm afraid they didn't exactly take to one another, did they?'

'Caroline seemed in an odd mood.' Fiona Marshall delved for cutlery. 'I've never known her so brittle – except just after the Gavin débâcle.'

'That's several years back now. But people have been attacking her over this idea of going into general practice. More than an idea, by now. They're advertising her post, and everyone's furious with her.'

'Would she have cleared off if Gavin had been around still?'

'No one's dared ask. But perhaps the pressure has been getting under her skin. She did seem edgy – and, after all, she has as much right as anyone else to go to hell in her own way. I'd better warn the troops to lay off her a bit.'

Meanwhile Caroline and Daniel were walking together across the square towards the big block of staff flats. Between them the silence was electric. Anything could have happened. Both of them knew it.

But Caroline lost her nerve. Muttering incoherently, as soon as they reached the west block she bolted through the swing doors and rushed upstairs. Daniel, on the pavement outside, walked purposefully along to the east block and his own flat, trying to deny the strange emptiness that had taken possession of him.

And for the next few weeks that was to be their pattern. A disjointed series of conversations, broken off by one of them just as they were showing signs of promise. And although on the surface no one could have appeared more confident than Daniel Harcourt, every time Caroline appeared to snub him, and dashed away – obviously, he could see, with better things on hand than standing around wasting time talking to him – he disintegrated. He continued, naturally, to show a tough, impenetrable personality, brusque and often downright rude, round the hospital. That he lacked a smooth bedside manner surprised no one. At Mortimer's they despised such fripperies, adopting a sincere, down-to-earth approach, which often, so the Central maintained, frightened their patients to death. Sir Graham Williamson's previous registrar, the story went, had had to do a reassuring round after the completion of his chief's tour, to convince patients panicked by the professor's academic dubiety and head shaking that they were not in fact booked for the mortuary within the week.

They'd expected a brilliant pedant, like Sir Graham, weighing every word, a textbook on legs, yet endowed with some sort of second sight that enabled him to astound them just when they were deciding they'd at last got his measure.

Daniel Harcourt astounded them all right. 'The man's more like a bloody surgeon,' they told one another, and it wasn't meant as a compliment. Enthusiastic, outgoing, aggressive, he turned Sir Graham's chilly ward rounds into battlefields, contradicting his chief left right and centre, boosting the patients' morale. He'd been Sir Graham's house physician a year or two back, so the dour

Scot must have known what he was in for, they commented, puzzled.

The dour Scot, of course, knew exactly what he was up to, as usual. He'd recognized Daniel's flair, and his intellectual capacity, from the beginning, had picked him out, and had been fighting resolutely since Daniel had first clerked for him to instil into him some of his own caution and balanced judgement. And he enjoyed his ward rounds no end with this argumentative clever youngster to stimulate him, and, he knew, bring out his best. They were a well-matched pair, and Sir Graham was fully aware of it.

He knew, too, something of the other side of Daniel's nature. He had seen below the surface to the hidden insecurity. He'd taken pains, too, to elicit his background, and since he was nothing if not thorough, he had amassed considerable detail about his junior. Daniel Harcourt was the son of a station master at a busy junction in the midlands. His father had left school at fourteen and had gone into the railway. He'd had five years in the army in wartime, coming out as a sergeant, and had returned with satisfaction to his wife and his small terrace house. It was he who had insisted that Daniel should go to the grammar school when opportunity offered, but he'd seen no further than that. Daniel would be educated until he was eighteen, a great advance, and he'd find a good job in a bank or an insurance company. When the question of university came up, Daniel was on his own. His parents couldn't offer any backing. They were stunned at the prospect. 'It's not for our sort of folk, laddie,' his father warned him. 'You've done very well as it is. But enough's enough. Pack it in now and be thankful. Or you'll find yourself out of your depth.' Not an attitude to inspire the young Daniel with confidence. But the school did that, and he'd embarked on his preclinical years in faraway London.

And, exactly as his father had predicted, he found himself out of his depth.

It was always happening. Sir Graham Williamson, who saw further than most, knew it. But no one else.

He was out of his depth now. At the Central, though, they never for a minute supposed it. After all, he'd arrived full of confidence, as registrar to one of their great men, and while already they were beginning to respect him, perhaps even fear him a little, that he might be experiencing any insecurity himself never crossed their minds – Caroline's least of all. She was far too busily engaged in repairing the gaps in her own armour-plating.

For both of them, though, the days were magical. Hope met Caroline at every corner. Anticipation gleamed behind each door. To walk the familiar corridors of the Central was to live hourly with excitement. At any moment Daniel, lanky, dark-haired and untidy, would materialize, his white coat hiding the shambles of the suit beneath. Often he'd have his houseman, Johnny Waller, with him, and he'd be arguing, jabbing his Biro at some reading in a report from the path lab or the radiology department. He'd look up, and a brief dialogue would ensue, often banal to the point of absurdity, but leaving a glow over the day. 'Hullo,' he'd say. 'Where are you off to?'

'Just up to the ward,' Caroline might answer. 'To check on that new admission.'

'As soon as I've cleared up this small problem I'll be up there myself,' he'd say.

'See you, then,' Caroline would say cheerfully, as if to do so would be mere routine. They'd continue on their separate ways, both of them walking on air and about three feet taller.

Even Claridge's Grill or the roof-top restaurant at the Hilton could not have pleased them more than Sister's office, where they often sat together, sorting out case notes or drinking tea after a ward round. One evening after a long day it was the scene of their first assignation. Daniel had been up most of the previous night, and his face, usually so alert and humorous, was drawn and pallid, his eyelids heavy over those incredible dark eyes that invariably had such an inexplicable effect on Caroline. He finished signing path forms, leant back in his chair, stretched, and mumbled almost incomprehensibly, 'Care for a cup of tea?'

Caroline, though, hanging on his every word, caught it. 'Love one,' she said immediately, unaware how ferociously he was cursing himself inwardly. Surely he could have offered her something more interesting than tea? However, oddly enough, she seemed to have accepted, so they'd better make tracks.

They were out of luck. As they reached the door, the telephone rang. Casualty. Could one of them come down, stat. They went together, and found that one of the local general practitioners had arrived with a four-year-old boy in his car. He'd been looking after him at home, treating him for a feverish cough. At teatime he'd been going along all right. But the mother, agitated, had rung him at the beginning of evening surgery, and he'd gone along to find the child going blue, and struggling for breath.

When Caroline and Daniel reached him, the small boy was threshing about wildly. His colour was an evil mauve. The casualty officer, together with the family doctor and a staff nurse, Prue Macfarlane, was attempting to give him oxygen, but the child, panic-stricken, fought them too hard for this to have any effect.

'We're getting nowhere, so we've sent for the consultant anaesthetist,' the casualty officer told them.

'A direct laryngoscopy is what we need to do, stat.' Caroline said.

'If we can.' Daniel was grim. And rightly so. Not a hope. The small boy was far too obstreperous, and his colour worse with every breath he failed to take.

But the senior registrar in anaesthetics arrived just in time and saved the day – and almost certainly the child's life. He succeeded in getting the oxygen into him, with an anaesthetic, halothane, and almost within seconds the little boy's struggling ceased as if by magic, as he slipped into unconsciousness and, to everyone's enormous relief, became pink again.

Now they were able to look through the laryngoscope, only to find his throat so swollen that, although he was able to breathe, and they knew his throat could not, in fact, be blocked, none of them could see any sign of an opening between the vocal cords.

Prue Macfarlane – a fascinating blonde, pursued by all the males in the hospital, who happened also to be renowned for her efficiency – as usual one step ahead, now had a splendid selection of endotracheal tubes ready for them.

The anaesthetist picked out a suitable-size tube and proffered it to Caroline. 'This is a difficult one,' he said. 'Would you like a quick try? If not I'll do it.'

'Please,' Caroline said, and took the tube from him. Taking on problem tasks like this was the way to learn, and normally she would have been grateful for the opportunity. This evening, though, she was nervous. For some reason, she was unable to bear the thought of failing in front of Daniel.

He caught her tension. 'Or shall I try?' he suggested.

'No, I will.' Caroline snapped the words out, furious with herself, and the anaesthetist, who'd heard a rumour that Caroline and the new registrar from Mortimer's didn't seem to get on, was able to endorse this from his own observation.

Meanwhile Caroline, unaware, was probing gently, even Daniel forgotten as she lived in the tips of her fingers and in her eyes, peering down the throat of the unconscious child, and to her relief found the opening, and slipped the tube through. Everyone heaved a sigh of thankfulness.

'Good. I'll stop the halothane now,' the anaesthetist said, 'and we'll keep him under with nitrous oxide and oxygen.'

The general practitioner thanked them and went back to his interrupted surgery, Prue Macfarlane went off to reassure the mother, who at last drank the cup of tea they'd provided for her, and Caroline and Daniel took the little boy to paediatric intensive care, though another hour went by before they felt they could leave him – he was pink and breathing nicely by then, they'd started him on ampicillin, and even his mum had stopped agonizing over him and was worrying instead about the neighbour who'd been landed with her other two.

'Remember that cup of tea we were going to have?' Daniel asked.

'Is it still on offer?'

'Very much so. Unless you'd rather have something a good deal stronger?'

'No, tea is what I'd like. I've the sort of thirst that gallons of tea might just about quench. Nothing else.'

'You were good, you know,' he told her as they walked along the square. 'I don't think I'd have been able to get straight through like that.'

She was pleased out of all proportion. 'I was dead scared I was going to fail,' she said honestly.

Reliving the episode from start to finish, they entered Daniel's flat. 'Sure you want tea?' he asked again. He longed to be able to offer her champagne, or age-old brandy, but the sole alternative to tea that he had in stock was a pint of milk and the end of a jar of Nescafé.

'Positive,' she assured him. Anything out of an old chipped mug with Daniel would be nectar. At last she'd found herself in his pad. She prowled round. How different it was from her own flat. Untidy. Book filled. And somehow unmistakably masculine, making her own careful arrangements seem prissy.

'Sorry it's in such a mess,' he said, coming in from the adjoining kitchen, hastily clearing piles of papers and journals, mixed with books, drug advertisements and unanswered mail, off the sofa.

'It's nice,' Caroline assured him inadequately.

He went away again, returned with a mug of tea.

'Thanks. You know, I shall be sorry to leave all this behind,' she added, to her own surprise.

Daniel wanted to tell her she needed her head examining to contemplate leaving the Central and a career of the sort hers promised to be, but today was a milestone, the first occasion she had entered his flat and sat alone with him in peace and content, away from demands and interruptions. He wasn't going to spoil it by lecturing her.

What did spoil things was the telephone, calling him back to the ward, where Johnny had an emergency on his hands.

Caroline went back to her own flat, so neat and tidy, to ask herself for the first time what the entire department had unavailingly been demanding for the past six months. How could she think of leaving?

She wanted to stay at the Central. With Daniel.

But she wasn't some volatile adolescent, she reminded herself firmly. She was not only qualified in medicine, but well on the way to being reasonably senior and experienced. She'd decided, calmly and for sound reasons, on the course her career should follow, and she couldn't turn it upside down simply because one day she suddenly imagined herself in love with a man with extraordinary eyes.

In any case, she'd had the love-and-passion scene. She knew all about it. With Gavin she'd had wonderful, unforgettable days – God knows she'd tried hard enough to forget them. But Gavin was in California living with Elaine, and must never be thought of. Too much hurt there. Too much pain.

Jerkily she walked to the window, looked down on to the square below.

Surely it couldn't all be beginning again?

She knew it was. This possession by another human being, this sudden flowering into brilliance of each second they were together, the intense value attached to every sight and sound, and the sense of imminent delight – she knew it, recognized it too well. And it frightened her to death. Because it meant, inevitably, pain and loss, misery and heartbreak.

As second-year students, she and Gavin had fallen in love. Together they had bashed the textbooks, eaten, taken exams and compared results, gone forward to their clinical years in the hospital, worked in the wards as dressers and clerks. From the beginning, they'd been sensible about the future. Or, to be truthful, they'd told each other they were going to be sensible. No strings, no emotional blackmail. Not for them. No marriage plans, either. They had to qualify and embark on their careers. Then, after qualification, they were both so appallingly, unendingly tired. This was when everything went bad on them. But, always, Caroline trusted their love. It was deep and longstanding. With so much between them nothing could go seriously wrong. In her own mind she was certain that they were destined for marriage, and medical partnership too.

Unexpectedly Gavin was offered a year's fellowship in

the States, at the Johns Hopkins. He had to take it up, of course. It was too good an offer to miss. Caroline tried hard to be glad for his sake, and they had a farewell party in the King's Head. The next morning she went to see him off at Heathrow.

She didn't know how to bear his absence. Over five years since she'd been alone, like this, and her life, though busy and full, was empty. She'd never felt so desolate. She treasured each one of Gavin's letters – and his memory, too, forgetting his faults, all their differences, and longing for the day of his return. Work, she thought, saved her from breakdown. Hard work in the wards and clinics, and flogging the books in any free moment meant that although she longed for Gavin she didn't have much space in her day for thinking about him. At night, sleep was apt to overtake her before she'd had more than a second or two to dwell on his lost companionship. Once or twice a day she'd think briefly, achingly, of him as she passed the seat in the square they'd so often used for revision, or when she sat, alone – among friends, of course, but without Gavin, alone – in the King's Head, talking after a heavy clinic.

In the autumn, when she was expecting him back, almost counting the days, the news came. He'd had a holiday in the States, been to San Francisco and Los Angeles. Had a whale of a time.

Not alone, either.

Her friends discovered this before Caroline. At first she couldn't understand the odd glances, the sudden breaks in conversation when she joined them, the strained silences. And then she began to notice that they seemed to be sorry for her. And angry about something.

When the next letter came she found out why. Gavin had been offered another post in the States, and he'd taken it. He'd be there for a further year, at least. He might even settle there. He was going around with this girl, Elaine, he'd been on holiday with. She was great. Caroline would be sure to like her.

Determined to be civilized, to make it easy for him, Caroline wrote back at once saying how glad she was about the post. She was sure, too, she'd like Elaine, and looked forward to meeting her. The falsity of writing such an untruthful letter to Gavin of all people brought the facts inescapably home to her. They were finished. It had ended. She had imagined their love would endure throughout a lifetime, but already it was over. Gone.

She turned a stony front to the hospital. At all costs no one must guess how lost she was.

But they all knew. Each time anyone mentioned Gavin's name, their eyes crossed and someone switched the conversation fast.

Four years now since Gavin had left for the Johns Hopkins, she thought, staring down into the square, remembering, vowing she wasn't going to go all through that again. Not with Daniel or anyone. Not at any price. This excitement that possessed her, this new insecurity when Daniel was around, was terrifying. She'd found out how much pain it could bring. Never again.

Down in Stonebridge her days would be organized, calm, occupied. And her father, whom she loved dearly, was expecting her, hanging on grimly for her return, coming home each night to an empty house, alone all evening with memories of her mother. They must be like her own memories of Gavin. Except that her father's extended over thirty-five years. Unbearable. She had to be with him.

2

Caroline and Daniel

'I have to go home,' she said. 'I can't get out of it now.'
She was talking to Daniel. They'd been sitting in Sister's
office drinking coffee and sorting out admissions and discharges, and then, as they walked along the corridor towards the stairs, Daniel had said, 'How about a meal
this evening? Would you by any chance be free?'

Caroline had no idea what she'd answered, except that
she knew he was calling for her at eight o'clock. She
showered and changed, smothering herself in ludicrously
expensive body lotion that she normally hoarded frugally,
drowning herself in toilet water, shrugging herself into her
favourite dress, a soft Indian cotton, and only at that point
stopping to ask herself what in the world she supposed
she was up to – anyone would think, she told herself
furiously, that you were expecting him to strip you to
the skin within five minutes.

Promptly at eight o'clock, before she'd been able to
work out the answer to that, he was on the doorstep,
looking unusually immaculate. Could he by any stretch
of the imagination have gone so far as to press his suit?
He looked wary, a fraction on edge, and for the first time
Caroline grasped that he might be as unnerved as she
was herself.

'Nice place,' he said formally.

'The same as yours,' she told him, and then wondered
anxiously if he would think she was implying that his
could easily be nice too, but emphatically failed to be.

22

'I suppose it must be,' he agreed.

Apparently he hadn't taken offence.

'Except that my hall is at the end of the room, and yours at the side,' she volunteered brightly.

After this they worked out with obsessional care the exact geography of their two flats. This accomplished, they switched to the route they should follow to reach Giovanni's, a hundred yards away. Giovanni's achieved, they discussed what to eat and drink, and then at last, while devouring the food, the cases they were discharging. This endured until coffee.

Caroline was despairing. They might as well have been sexless, a couple of busy physicians snatching a quick hour to sort out the ward. And she knew it was wrong for both of them, not what either of them wanted. Surely she was capable of cutting through this meaningless chatter? Of communicating?

Daniel paid the bill, and then, as they left Giovanni's, asked if she'd care for a bit of a walk. 'Round the square, say?'

'Oh, I'd love it.'

They strolled along St Anne's Square, and he asked, abruptly, 'Worried about leaving here, are you?'

'Well, yes, I am,' Caroline admitted. 'But I have to go home. I can't get out of it now.'

'D'you want to, then?'

'Yes,' she heard herself say. 'I suppose I do. In a way.'

'What sort of way?'

Unthinkable to announce 'I want to stay at the Central with you'. She embarked instead on a long rigmarole about the past and the future, her mother, her father, the practice at Stonebridge. Daniel listened, and made useful, down-to-earth comments. It never occurred to him that anywhere inside Caroline's cool collected self, swinging trimly along at his side as they tramped, unnoticing, round

23

St Anne's Square for nearly an hour, was a lost girl crying out, and falling every moment deeper in love with him.

He knew himself to be in love with her – but he didn't rate his chances highly. He knew all about Gavin. Registrars and housemen, they all remembered him. Caroline had taken a hard knock, they told Daniel, and wasn't over it yet.

'It turned her into a career girl pure and simple,' Andrew Marshall had said. 'After Gavin had gone to the Johns Hopkins she got the Membership first try – '

Daniel, who'd also gained the Membership of the Royal College of Physicians at the first attempt, was perhaps less impressed than many others would have been at this particular nugget of information.

' – and we all began to realize what an incredible waste it was going to be if she disappeared into general practice. But there it is, she turns a deaf ear to anything we say. Great loss, though.'

'I agree,' Daniel said curtly, and changed the subject.

Andrew drew the wrong conclusion. Daniel had no time for Caroline, he decided. The hospital agreed with him, and with some reason, for with each other Caroline and Daniel continued to behave oddly. Their conversation was uneasy and tense. Their moods were erratic. And, their companions considered, just as the anaesthetist had said, they were locked in unending rivalry, perpetually trying to score off one another. That this was the uncertain start of a love affair occurred to no one.

Meanwhile Caroline went through with her plans to return to Stonebridge, Dr Berkeley, grumbling, interviewed candidates to replace her, an appointment was made, and finally Caroline handed over her work. That night the department threw a farewell party for her. This was a huge success, enjoyed enormously by everyone except Caroline who, looking sensational in a floating scrap of flame-coloured chiffon purchased extravagantly in the depths of despair, felt as though she was going to her death.

'I wish you weren't going,' Daniel ventured, around midnight, when they found themselves standing together in a corner of Andrew's sitting room temporarily forgotten while an argument raged over what precisely the prof had in mind when he'd summarily dismissed Andrew's perfectly sound proposal on the treatment of coeliac disease.

'I wish I wasn't,' Caroline agreed, her eyes melting above her glass.

'I shall miss you.' Daniel issued this statement like a challenge.

'I shall miss you too,' Caroline told him, in hardly more than a whisper. She looked terrified, and at that moment Daniel understood her, for the first time read her clearly. He dumped his glass on the window-sill.

'You will?' he asked, his own eyes brilliant. 'Let me take that from you.' He removed her glass from her now trembling hand, and put it with his own. 'Come on,' he said, a hand under her arm. 'Out.'

His hand was not in the least like Gavin's. Daniel's touch was a new experience, and Caroline was filled by a poignant longing simply to stand there for ever while he went on holding her arm. Instead she put her own hand over his – and that proved to be yet another new sensation. She shivered, and somehow they seemed to be on the stairs outside the flat, locked together with precision, as though they'd been doing this a hundred times a day for ten years.

Daniel broke violently away. 'My flat or yours?' he asked.

'I – I don't know. Doesn't matter.' Caroline's lips were bruised and she was shaking.

'Come on.' He dragged her after him down the stairs and out into the square.

'Mine's nearer,' Caroline offered breathlessly.

'Right.'

Up the familiar stairs, and in.

'Oh my God,' Daniel said, and took her into his arms again. 'I've wanted this for months. What a load of time we've wasted.'

Momentarily Caroline drew back, and traced the line of his brow, and then of his lips, slowly, passionately. 'Oh, Daniel,' she said. 'I love you. I love you so much.'

His arms were like iron, his lips hard and devouring against hers. She lay back, and felt the flame-coloured chiffon tear. It meant nothing. Only this flaring excitement and utter certainty counted. Daniel's lean hard body lay along her own, they clung together wordlessly, and in the midst of the wild sweeping joy she knew a sense of utter peace and security.

Daniel jerked himself up on one elbow. 'Hell,' he said. 'I haven't let them know where I am, and I'm taking Andrew's calls. Supposed to be.'

Wordlessly, Caroline gestured at the telephone.

Daniel picked it up. 'Dr Harcourt. If you want me you can get me on Dr Milne's extension.' With his free hand he explored the back of her neck. And then his face changed. 'Oh, have you? Yes, we must have been walking across. Does he? I see. I'll be right over.'

It wasn't possible. 'You don't have to –'

'Afraid so. Only some minor panic of Johnny's, I dare say. I'll be back.'

'Any time.'

'Sure?'

'Absolutely any time.'

He kissed her, and was gone. For an unknown period that could as easily have been four minutes as four hours,

Caroline lay savouring her joy, waiting confidently for Daniel to return. When it at last struck her that whatever was keeping him could not be some minor panic, she lay there still, putting off the moment of looking at her watch, half drifting into sleep, half thinking about Daniel. When, finally, she checked the hour, she found it was nearly three in the morning. Rousing herself, she ran a bath and at last, perfumed, hair brushed, turned out the lights except for the small reading lamp beside her divan, and went, tidily and hopefully, to bed, filled with anticipation still and not expecting for one second to drop off to sleep.

She awoke in a grey dawn.

No sign of Daniel. Had he been kept in the ward all night? Or had he simply decided that it was too late to return, no matter what she'd said? Or was it that he no longer felt any inclination to make love to her? But this possibility was too incredible to keep her awake, and she drifted into a happy sleep.

At seven-thirty her alarm woke her. A chilly, drizzling morning, and now her mood had changed, was as grey and dismal as the new day. Had she and Daniel been happy together last night? Difficult to believe. In any case, last night had nothing to say to this morning. Today she left the Central and returned to Stonebridge. The prospect was hateful. Just as they had been telling her for months, she must be out of her mind. Why in God's name had she never listened to them?

Too late now. The decision had been taken, the wheels had turned, and she had no alternative. A fine time to come to her senses. What she had to do this morning was to complete her packing, check the flat inventory with the office, empty the fridge and defrost, have the meter read, put her books into cases for Pickfords to collect, and then ring for a taxi to take her to Waterloo with her hand luggage.

Dully, she washed, pulled on jeans and a shirt, filled the kettle for a quick mug of Nescafé.

Eight o'clock, and a ring at the doorbell. The man from the electricity board to read the meter, no doubt.

But it wasn't. It was Daniel. She fell into his arms, babbling joyfully, hugging him ferociously with excitement at having him with her again. Drawn and unshaven, his suit rumpled, his shirt stained, he'd clearly been up in the ward throughout the night.

'Sorry,' he said, when they at last disentangled themselves. 'Couldn't make it before.'

'Hard night?'

'Busy, fairly.' He was laconic. 'The little leukaemia boy.'

'And?'

'Still with us. Just. I don't know if we're going to manage to keep him going and get a remission, though. Still hoping we may, but – ' He shook his head, and his eyes were bleak. 'Time will show.'

Caroline nodded. It would be touch and go for days, even weeks, yet. But she wouldn't be around to know the result. Hurriedly she pushed this thought to the back of her mind. 'Breakfast,' she said crisply. 'I'll make some for us both. You must be starving. Breakfast and then some sleep is what you need.'

'There'll be time for that this afternoon. Perhaps. Old man's ward round this morning. I must tidy up for it. Shave, too.' He ran a hand over his chin.

'And have breakfast,' Caroline persisted.

'That too.'

'Have it here with me.'

'Great. I'll slip over to my place and shave – back in, say, fifteen minutes. All right?'

'Perfectly,' she assured him, and kissed the bristles adoringly. He held her to him, and suddenly there was no more fatigue in him. 'Couldn't we just – ' he began.

The doorbell rang.

This time it was the man to read the meter.

'Back shortly,' Daniel said.

Caroline saw the meter reader off, and began to plan the most magnificent breakfast of her life.

Until she opened the denuded fridge. She'd been deliberately using up her stocks, and it contained less than half a pint of milk, an almost empty packet of Flora margarine, one cracked egg and about an inch of cheese. In the bread bin was the heel of a loaf.

Recklessly, she pounded down the stairs and along the road, round the corner to the delicatessen. She bought fresh hot rolls, butter, milk, six eggs and half a pound of bacon. She tore back to the flat, and was composedly grilling bacon and frying eggs when Daniel returned, groomed and smelling of after-shave, his crisp hair damp and flatter than usual, little tendrils curling endearingly about his forehead and his ears. He sniffed contentedly, held her round the waist from behind, and rubbed his newly soft cheek against hers. 'You have the right ideas about breakfast,' he told her.

It is not altogether easy to eat rolls and butter accompanied by bacon and egg, while holding hands and looking into the depths of your partner's eyes. They managed it.

Another ring at the doorbell.

Caroline's next-door neighbour, a pathologist, to say a final goodbye and ask if there was anything she could do. Her jaw dropped as she spotted Daniel munching away in the background and she retreated. 'Must rush,' she said unconvincingly. 'Give me a ring if there's anything you want done.'

Caroline returned to the table, amused. 'Something tells me she jumped to conclusions.'

'All round the hospital by coffee time, I shouldn't wonder.' Daniel was amiable. 'Never mind, we'll lose no opportunity to make today's erroneous conclusion fact, shall we?'

'None at all.'

He glanced at his watch. 'If it wasn't four minutes to nine, so that I've precisely two minutes to reach the main entrance and greet the prof with my shining morning face, I'd take you up on that,' he said. 'As it is, I'm off. Look after yourself.'

'And you.'

They exchanged last kisses tasting of bacon, and Caroline watched until the lanky, loose-jointed figure of her new love, her only love, her forever love, passed the corner of the stairs. She stood in the doorway listening to his footsteps receding, heard the swing doors bang behind him.

3

Daniel and Robert

No looking back, Caroline told herself peremptorily as she woke the next morning in her own room at Burvale. No odious comparisons. General practice in Stonebridge was not going to be anything like the department of child health at the Central, and she must face the fact and be ready to lead an entirely different sort of existence.

The first shock was to find that her mother's two partners, Dr Hector Armstrong and Dr Marjorie Evans, had inaugurated an appointment system in Dr Armstrong's house, the Hollies, in the centre of the town, and proposed to hold all surgeries there. Throughout Caroline's childhood, morning and evening surgery had been held at Burvale, and one of her plans had been to start seeing patients there again, so that the empty house would come alive once more.

'Must move with the times, after all, Caroline,' Dr Armstrong said jovially. He was a big, genial man, and the patients were inclined to worship him, most of them preferring him to Dr Evans, who was quiet and self-contained, but had, so Caroline's mother asserted, more brains and diagnostic flair in her little finger than Dr Armstrong in his great bald pate.

'I know originally we moved the surgeries here as a temporary measure when your mother collapsed,' Dr Evans added. 'But it's worked out very well, and we've decided to go on with it.'

'We've decided.' That was another shock. Dr Armstrong and Dr Evans took the decisions. Dr Alan Peterson and Dr Caroline Milne were not junior partners, but assistants.

Caroline supposed she'd been hopelessly naïve and unbusinesslike. Her mother had always referred, half humorously at first, admittedly, to Caroline as 'my future junior partner', and it had never occurred to her that Dr Armstrong and Dr Evans, lifelong friends of the family, might not share this assumption, that there might not be a junior partnership awaiting her any time she liked to take it up. Now, too late, she found herself no more than an assistant 'with a view', as the jargon had it.

Perhaps she should have protested. But before doing any complaining, she had to make up her own mind. Did she want partnership, or did an assistant's post suit her perfectly? Would she be able, as soon as her father was reasonably comfortably established, to say a thankful farewell? At least, though, having returned home, she must give Stonebridge a fair trial.

But she didn't. She couldn't. Her thoughts were of Daniel, the longing to be back in the Central with him overpowering and ever-present. Two hundred miles, and two separate, demanding jobs kept them firmly apart. Each weekend they planned to meet, yet a month went by, and they'd not set eyes on one another. Every other weekend Caroline was on call for the practice, and one of her free Sundays happened to be her father's birthday. That evening she laid on a dinner party, though the guests were really a working group from his office, consisting of his own junior partner, Jeremy Watson, an efficient, likeable young accountant who'd been a tower of strength when Peggy Milne died so suddenly, the local solicitor and his wife, and Ginny Barnton, the senior secretary at Milne and Watson's. Hardly a scintillating occasion, though Caroline had always got on well with Ginny, and, now she herself was living in Stonebridge, looked forward to seeing more of her. In fact, on the evening of the dinner party they arranged to meet for a shopping expedition to the nearest large town, Broomhurst, on Caroline's next free afternoon.

The shopping expedition was for the purpose of buying – if she could, in provincial Broomhurst – something to wear for the Central ball, a dressy affair. Daniel had invited her to go with him, and Caroline had already cleared the date with Alan Peterson, who would take her calls, and with Dr Armstrong too. He had been kindly, though distinctly patronizing, and she suspected he thought of her still as a teenager. It was a pity, in view of this, that her excitement over the ball proved impossible to hide. She felt, correctly, that it confirmed him in his opinion that she was a slip of a girl with her head full of young men.

One young man, of course. Daniel. But Dr Armstrong didn't see it like that. Caroline had been out with Jeremy Watson who, returning the Milnes' hospitality, took Caroline and her father, with Ginny Barnton again, to a meal at a hotel on the Broomhurst road. Dr Armstrong took up the attitude that she was playing one young man off against the other, jaunting off to London to a ball now, with a different date. Caroline smiled determinedly, and, her mind in the Central with Daniel, exchanged heavy-handed old-world repartee with Dr Armstrong.

She went up to Waterloo by train, and took a taxi to the Marshalls' flat, where they were to have dinner. Fiona greeted her. 'No one's here yet,' she said. 'I expect there's some sort of flap on, and they'll all be held up. Typical. But the meal won't spoil – I learnt my lesson years ago.'

Caroline shook out her dress – Broomhurst had come up to scratch – Fiona admired the drifting folds of beige and white gossamer chiffon, and went off to the kitchen again while Caroline changed, and thought about Daniel. Fiona was thinking about him too, as she tore up lettuce for prawn cocktails. Daniel and Caroline. What a turn-up for the books that had been. But would it last? Andrew thought not. That was a lovely dress Caroline had bought for the ball, though. She'd look fantastic in it. What would Daniel make of that?

At this moment he arrived, resplendent in a new midnight blue velvet jacket. Fiona, admitting him, blinked, and did her best to further the course of true love. If that was what it was. 'Caroline's arrived,' she said. 'But no one else, so far. I'm tied up in the kitchen for a while, so go in and join her.'

Caroline had heard him come, of course. She was standing by the window – that window where it had all begun – her heart pounding. Daniel came in, ignored her lovely dress, and took her straight into his arms. They clung together, and life was as wonderful, as ecstatic, as they had both remembered.

For about three seconds. And then Andrew – who, unlike Fiona, had no thoughts to spare for the course of true love – came roaring in with half the department behind him, who all surged round Caroline like a rugger scrum.

From that moment the evening flew by. Dinner at the Marshalls' was followed by an all-too-brief interval of dancing, when Daniel was able to snatch only two dances with Caroline, who was claimed, in turn, by Dr Walter Berkeley, Sir Graham Williamson (used to Scottish reels, and nimble on his narrow feet, unlike Dr Berkeley, who bumbled around and trod on her toes), Andrew Marshall and half a hundred registrars and housemen who'd known her far longer than he had. He was forced to concentrate on doing his duty by Lady Williamson, Fiona and the sisters and staff nurses from the ward and outpatients.

Back, in fact, to the old days of catching Caroline's eye across a sea of heads.

Midnight supper was to be in Dr Berkeley's house in nearby St Anne's Passage, a tall Georgian, book-filled house of considerable charm, whose ownership had enabled Wily Walter – as he was known throughout the hospital – to steal a march on his director, who might have been expected to be their host. But Sir Graham lived near Mortimer's, fifteen minutes' drive away, and his home had to be ruled out, so Walter Berkeley, who took his rivalry with Sir Graham exceedingly seriously, had been overjoyed to step in and invite them all back for a champagne supper. He had the greatest respect for Sir Graham's intellect, but he was hardly an all-round man, Wily Walter was found of saying darkly. Mortimer's was all very well, he'd not attempt to deny they did some good work there from time to time, but a Mortimer's background could never compare with the Central, could it?

As witness the champagne supper. Sir Graham would have done it on Asti Spumante or Veuve du Vernay, wouldn't they agree? Caroline – whom Dr Berkeley insisted on making his special care, turning on her a devoted attention she'd never rated as his registrar – was forced to admit he was right. The party, too, went with a swing, and didn't even begin to break up until well after three. It was nearly four when Caroline succeeded in extricating herself, pointing out that she had to collect her case from the Marshalls' and catch the 5.15 a.m. train back to Stonebridge. She and Daniel went back with Andrew and Fiona, and were invited to stay and drink tea – 'although it will be a bit of a come-down, I'm afraid'. Caroline, though, thought she'd better make at once for Waterloo, as she might not be able to pick up a taxi easily at that hour, even at the Central.

35

'None of us dare drive you,' Andrew said. 'Not with all that champagne swilling around inside.'

'I'll walk you,' Daniel offered. 'If you're not too tired.'

Of course she wasn't. And so at last they were alone, walking through the deserted squares and the empty streets, and across Waterloo Bridge in the pale dawn. A magic walk – but a hurried one, and Caroline caught the train with two minutes to spare, and leant out of the window, dishevelled and luminously beautiful in clouds of chiffon, and clung to Daniel's hands as though for ever.

'I can't bear to go,' she whispered.

'I can't bear to let you.'

'Come down for your first free weekend.'

'Nothing I'd like better.'

Caroline prepared carefully for this weekend, arranging for Alan Peterson to take her calls on Saturday evening and all day on Sunday. Daniel was coming down by train, and would be at the station at 12.45 p.m. on Saturday.

She saw to his room, even picking flowers for the chest of drawers, though she didn't suppose he was likely to notice them, and planned the weekend's menus with Mrs Gooch, who came to Burvale every other day to prepare their main meals.

But the worst happened. The local midwife called Caroline out soon after breakfast, to an outlying cottage, almost derelict, where a young unmarried mother had holed up. She had booked herself in nowhere at all for her confinement, had made no preparations for the baby. She'd only been able to summon help by calling out to the milkman, doing his round earlier than usual so that he could reach home in time for 'Grandstand' on the box. The girl was undernourished and, both Caroline and the midwife thought, had been on drugs, the cottage was

36

squalid and insanitary and, to cap it all, it was a breech presentation. Caroline and the midwife fought hard to produce a puny infant, unable to snatch even a few minutes to drive to the nearest telephone to call the obstetric flying squad from Broomhurst – who were the outfit they really needed. At last, though, the infant safely delivered, Caroline drove to the farm two miles down the road to telephone for the ambulance to take mother and baby to hospital. She waited at the cottage with the midwife until the ambulancemen arrived – raising their eyebrows at the state of the cottage. Caroline and the midwife commiserated with one another, and drove off homewards in search of hot baths.

Meanwhile Daniel, realizing that Caroline must have been held up on a call, had enquired the way to Burvale, and been told it was a goodish walk and he needed the station taxi. In this he was driven up to the Milnes' front door.

Burvale was an Edwardian villa, bay-windowed and ivy-covered, sitting comfortably among ample lawns and shrubberies, very different from the red-brick terrace in which Daniel had been raised. The contrast jolted him – until then he'd been thinking only of Caroline and not at all about her background.

The old-fashioned bell pealed, and out to meet him, not in the least welcoming, came Robert Milne. 'Oh,' he said. 'I suppose you must be that friend of my daughter's. You'd better come in. Don't know where she's got to – been out since breakfast.' He led the way into a gloomy hall, paved with black and white tiles that reverberated under Daniel's tread, so that he began to wonder if he had accidentally come in mountaineering boots. Robert Milne remarked decisively, 'You'll want to go to your room. Have a wash,' so that Daniel, already undermined, felt exactly like a grubby schoolboy who'd failed to arrive clean and tidy for an interview with the headmaster. They climbed, in silence, a wide flight of stairs to a half-landing itself about three times the size of Daniel's bedroom at home, and on up to an upper landing flooded with light from a glass dome in the roof. Robert Milne opened one or two doors, shutting them again with a discouraging 'Not here', 'Nor here', and then, happily, stumbled on the bedroom Caroline had prepared. 'Ah.' He cheered up. 'She must mean you to sleep here. Bed's made up. Flowers, too. Doesn't put flowers in my room, does she? Eh?'

No reply to this angry enquiry came to Daniel. He knew how to deal with irascible consultants, though he'd had to learn the hard way – from his failures. But he had no notion how to cope, in this vast and forbidding house, with this stranger, Caroline's father – who looked, to make it somehow more impossibly difficult, astonishingly like Caroline. He dumped his case, and heard himself mumbling like a retarded oaf.

'Come down when you're ready,' Robert ordered. 'Have to try and find you some luncheon, shan't I?' He was as much unnerved as Daniel. This was the registrar from the Central Caroline kept mentioning, her face changing completely every time she spoke of him. This was the strange young man from London who held Caroline's heart, who was going to steal her away, make her leave home again. As if in a nightmare, Robert Milne could see it happening. Peggy, who had been warmth and comfort, who had understood his ways, who'd become part of him, had gone without warning, and he'd found himself lost, alone in this house that had always hummed with activity. Now there were no patients coming and going, no telephone ringing from early until late, and he couldn't bear to come into the emptiness, leaving it until the last possible moment each evening. At last, though, Caroline had come home to live and work, and the telephone began to ring again, while at mealtimes she told him about her daily round, as her mother had always done. Existence was becoming bearable again, and though he'd warned himself that one day she was bound to marry he'd hoped it would not be for some years, and then only to another doctor in the town.

But now this stranger from London appeared, wanting, Robert was sure of it, to take Caroline away, back to the Central. And what's more, make no mistake, Caroline wanted to go. She was in love with the damned boy.

He pulled himself together. Caroline had her life to live. His own was past. He'd had his marriage, and he mustn't interfere with hers. He mustn't become possessive. He'd better be nice to Daniel Harcourt, and find him some luncheon, too.

He walked through to the kitchen, consulted the instructions Caroline always pinned to the cupboard door about the day's meals. Hearing Daniel's feet on the hall tiles, he called out to him.

Daniel followed the sound along a wide passage, through a green baize door, where another passage, stone-flagged and chilly, led off to right and left. Knife-sharpening noises came from the left, so he turned in that direction, and found his host preparing to cut into a joint of cold beef.

'This is what seems to be on the menu,' Robert informed him. He jerked his head at the note on the cupboard door, in what Daniel saw at once to be his absent beloved's familiar hand. He went over and scrutinized it.

'Can I do anything towards this meal, sir?' The head-master image persisting, the formal designation seemed called for.

Robert was in fact mollified by this mark of respect. At least the young man had a few manners about him.

39

'Salad,' he said. 'Can you concoct a salad? That's what Caroline intends us to eat – see for yourself – and I can't make a salad.'

Neither could Daniel. 'Well, I suppose,' he began doubtfully, 'I could wash some lettuce, and – '

'Should be ready washed. Usually is. Somewhere in the fridge. What I meant was, can you make a salad dressing, and toss the damned stuff?'

Daniel reddened. Tossing salad had never entered into his scheme of things. And he wasn't going to lie down and grovel about it, either. 'I usually have mayonnaise with it,' he said firmly.

'Mayonnaise? You can make that, can you?'

'No. I buy it. In a bottle.'

'Oh. Oh, really?' Robert paused in his carving, and regarded Daniel briefly with another headmaster's look, the sort shot across at you when you flunked an answer. 'I'm afraid we don't, as far as I know, possess any *bottled* mayonnaise,' Caroline's abominable parent informed him icily.

'Pity.' Daniel was determined not to be put down. 'Useful stuff.'

'I daresay it might be. However, I'm afraid today you'll have to make do with lettuce and tomato *au nature*, so to speak.'

At all costs, don't antagonize the old devil, Daniel reminded himself. 'Very nice, sir.' He opened the fridge and hunted around, as he'd been bidden, and found washed lettuce together with cucumber and tomatoes in the salad drawer, which he took over to the big kitchen table.

'Ah ha, good lad.' Robert brightened up. 'We'll just help ourselves and have it on the side of our plate, eh?'

Where did they usually have it, in heaven's name?

'And cut a chunk of cucumber.' Robert did this with

the carving knife, and offered a piece in a comparatively friendly manner.

Daniel took it. 'Knives and forks?' he asked.

'In the dining room.'

'Oh. Can't we just eat in here?' As soon as the words were halfway out Daniel knew they were a mistake. He'd done for himself now.

'Here? Certainly not. It's never been my custom to sit down and eat in the kitchen, and I don't intend to begin now.

'I just thought it might be simpler.' Daniel heard the apology in his voice, and was furious with himself.

'Perfectly simple to take our plates through to the dining room,' Robert said, suiting the action to the words.

Seething inwardly, Daniel followed him.

In a barnlike dining room a great oval mahogany table was placed at one end for three, with a wide array of plates, cutlery, glasses and little silver oddments. Uneasily, Daniel sat down.

By the time they'd progressed to cheese and then coffee, made in a Cona which Robert plugged in on the massive sideboard, both of them were feeling the strain, though they'd made strenuous efforts to reach one another. But they weren't on the same wavelength.

Caroline, returning from the cottage and her energetic and worrying delivery, hair falling over what she was well aware was a greasy, shiny face, shirt and jeans blood-stained and filthy, entered on to this scene of unmistakable estrangement. Tired and hungry, she was unable to deal with the two people she loved most sitting over their coffee, and plainly hating one another. That her father might have been less than cordial failed to occur to her – though it should have done – and instead she at once blamed Daniel for whatever had happened, supposing him to have displayed the characteristics he'd shown on

41

first arrival at the Central – aggression and impatience. Like an over-anxious mother rather than a daughter, she rushed to cherish Robert, whose undisguised misery since Peggy Milne's death Caroline felt as her responsibility day and night.

That Daniel might have been intimidated by both her father and her home never entered her head. Daniel, intimidated? Their love and mutual absorption, after all, was a very new birth, they'd spent amazingly little time together, and they knew extraordinarily little about one another except from intuition, which, that afternoon, had switched off. They were poles apart.

Daniel had been thankful to see Caroline at last – and then she stood there looking at him as though she hated him. He saw at once what it must be. From the beginning, she'd been determined to join her father in Stonebridge. And now, dug in here at home, in this pretentious mausoleum of a house, she was looking at him, Daniel Harcourt, as though he was something the cat brought in. She was asking herself what in the world had made her invite him here? He was a misfit, some lout she'd gone around with in her Central days.

'I must wash and change,' she announced, after hurried unfriendly greetings. 'And then have some food. I'm starving.' Perhaps after a meal this disaster would look different. 'Can you amuse yourself in the meantime?'

Amuse himself, for God's sake. He wasn't a child. Plainly, though, as far as Caroline was concerned, he was nothing more than a nuisance.

'I'll cut you some of this excellent beef, my dear,' her father said solicitously.

So while Robert went back along the passage to the kitchen, Daniel sauntered out of the dining room and into the large sitting room opposite, where he sat down and read the paper, feeling neglected and outcast. To clear the dining table did cross his mind, but he decided that would almost certainly be exactly the wrong thing to do again.

Caroline came down to beef and salad pressed on her by an unusually affectionate father. No sign of Daniel. She ate in the kitchen. For once her father didn't object, and she concluded he must have been so bullied by an overbearing Daniel that he had no spirit left to tick her off for behaviour she was well aware he disliked. Her heart bled for him.

After she'd eaten she felt much better, though in spite of her annoyance a good deal hurt by Daniel's continued absence. She wandered through to the dining room, where she'd last seen him, and found the table littered with the remains of the meal. In a flurry of irritation she cleared it. Did Daniel suppose the house ran itself? Useless to expect her father suddenly to become domesticated after all these years, but did Daniel too expect to be waited on hand and foot by female slaves?

In Edwardian days, when the house had been built, the clatter of crockery being washed was not meant to reach the drawing room, and Daniel, sitting there and ploughing doggedly through *The Times*, heard nothing. He assumed Caroline was avoiding him, and asked himself what the hell he could be doing, on his one free weekend of the month, two hundred miles from London, in this solitary grandeur, ignored by the Milnes, father and daughter. He was also unable to deny a fact that had been steadily creeping up on him. He was starting the department's cold. This had been decimating the staff for several weeks, and had chosen today to hit him.

The next morning his condition was unmistakable, and he apologized to Caroline, who dosed him with aspirin and the concoction that Central residents used when they had head colds – which was, Daniel assured her, all he had, though he was beginning to doubt this himself. He

43

suggested that perhaps he ought to go back to London soon after lunch. It was only fair to Caroline. 'And to you, sir,' he added. Robert had been coming and going all morning, interrupting any *tête-à-tête* with the indefatigability of a Victorian dowager on the prowl round a marriageable daughter of the house.

'Me?' he said. 'I don't matter. But I daresay Caroline won't want to catch it.'

'What time is the afternoon train?'

Robert told him at once, and Caroline drove him to the station to catch it, but they weren't, even then, to have any privacy. Robert saw to that. Implacably, now, adopting the air of ever-courteous host, he announced he'd see Daniel off, and sat himself alongside Caroline in Peggy Milne's old Rover. He accompanied them on to the platform, too, making, for the only occasion during Daniel's visit, almost sparkling small talk. When the train arrived he shut Daniel into it thankfully, and took Caroline's arm possessively as the train drew out.

Daniel was feeling almost too ill to care. His temperature was rocketing, his throat on fire, his eyes watering, and his head splitting. He couldn't make out what he was in for, but he doubted now if it was the cold the rest of them had been passing round. When he arrived at Waterloo he crawled straight into a taxi, and as soon as he reached his flat crept into bed and rang the medical registrar on call.

Within two hours he was warded.

4

Caroline and Jeremy

Daniel had measles. Of all the juvenile complaints to contract, at the very moment when you are having problems with a beautiful girl living in affluence in a large house with an irascible father, measles was about the least desirable. Spotty and ill – he took it badly – he received no sympathy. His colleagues fell about laughing. Andrew Marshall came to see him in the staff ward, where the duty medical registrar had consigned him that Sunday evening. He seemed, Daniel thought, a little odd in his manner, a glint of something amazingly akin to amusement lurking. 'Open mouth,' he'd commanded, and inserted a spatula. He'd withdrawn it, and now there could be no mistaking his attitude. Daniel's illness was funny. 'Koplik's spots, sure enough,' he announced gleefully. 'Measles, my lad. That's what you've got.'

At first Daniel had refused to believe it.

'Caroline's had it,' Andrew went on, grinning wickedly. 'So we needn't telephone her to put her in quarantine.' He regarded Daniel quizzically. 'Be thankful for small mercies, eh?'

Daniel found it impossible to be thankful for anything. Furious with himself and feeling very low, he wrote a stilted little thank-you note. As soon as she heard he had measles, no doubt she'd find it as funny as everyone else. Well, she wouldn't learn it from him. In any case, he had to face it, all was over between them. Robert Milne certainly had no intention of ever becoming his father-in-law, even if he himself could contemplate such a prospect with any sort of equanimity, which he could not. Spend the remainder of his days in close relationship to that old devil? Not if he knew it. Nor was there the faintest chance that he'd give up his career, his new post at the Central and all it might lead to, to follow snooty Dr Caroline Milne into general practice and play second fiddle all his life to her father. What did she imagine he was?

For nearly a week he was unable to read, had to lie cursing in a darkened room with streaming eyes, miserable, angry and frustrated. Then at last, as suddenly as the disease had hit him, it departed. He tottered shakily about the room, and in a day or two was able to leave for convalescence at home. His parents – though they too appeared to find the episode a huge joke – were delighted to have him. His mother – an excellent cook – fed him up, plying him all day long with snacks and titbits between enormous meals, while his father took him to the local and played darts against him. And Daniel saw as plainly as he'd done from his bed in the ward that to bring Caroline home to this little terraced house where his dad often washed in the scullery would be impossible. Equally unthinkable to take his parents to Burvale to meet Caroline's father. Robert Milne might try to patronize him, he could look after himself, but Daniel was damned if he was going to have the chance to look down his nose at the senior Harcourts.

He was desolate, but, his eyes having recovered, he was able to bury himself in his books and abjure women for life. That his illness might be responsible for this depressed and negative state of mind failed to occur to the rising young physician.

Meanwhile, in Stonebridge, Caroline, at first refusing to believe that anything so lovely and full of promise could have ended in silence, even after an admitted failure of a weekend, reminded herself bitterly that this was only a repeat performance. Like Gavin, Daniel had gone off her.

She could guess what had happened. Daniel had found Stonebridge too long a train journey and her father not sufficiently welcoming at the end of it, and, neither marriage nor an affair with her being practicable, he had faded away. Like Gavin. Only, of course, a good deal faster. While she herself must be the silly, devoted, faithful sort of girl who ate her heart out for disinterested men. To hell with them. She'd devote herself to general practice and looking after her father.

A praiseworthy aim, but it didn't exactly come off. On the one hand, she found it difficult to jettison Daniel's memory quite as fast as she planned, and, on the other, she didn't seem to be leading a quiet and cloistered existence.

Going about with her father involved spending time with Jeremy Watson, who was a kind young man, determined to do his best to ensure that his senior partner had few empty hours for grieving. For ever arranging dinners and lunches, he'd drop in too, at Burvale to invite Robert out for the odd pint, a walk over the downs, or a round of golf. If Caroline was in the house when he appeared, he asked her to come along. Since the alternative was to mope about, cross-examining herself about Daniel and his motivations, Caroline accepted and walked the golf course with them, explored the hotels and restaurants for miles around, and listened, for relaxation, to accountant's gossip instead of medical argument. Often they were a foursome, the two Milnes, Jeremy, and Ginny Barnton, and slowly, almost without awareness, Caroline and Jeremy began to take one another's companionship for granted.

Robert approved of their friendship. His attitude to

Jeremy was entirely different from his reaction to Daniel. Jeremy was his valued junior partner, a proven tower of strength, who had without complaint shouldered a mountain of work when he himself had been too distraught to deal with any problems but his own. Jeremy was like part of his family, and Robert wanted nothing more than to set a final seal on this by acquiring him as a son-in-law.

And as the year went by, the autumn of the Central ball giving way to winter and then spring, Caroline and Jeremy became an acknowledged pair, and although she continued to think about Daniel and wonder what had gone wrong between them, it was a problem from another life. Her days at the Central with him glittered in her memory, but those days were lost in the past. She'd had a duty to her father, and she knew she could never have turned her back on him and his overwhelming need of her. So she'd left the Central, and Daniel had not been sufficiently interested in her to travel two hundred miles to see her more than once. She had learnt to live without him, and now enjoyed a quite different existence. Another year, she decided, and her father and she would have settled down into their new routine together.

But that autumn brought a shock. Her father decided to marry again – Ginny Barnton. Early in the new year, the wedding took place, in Stonebridge Parish Church. Robert was a new man, cheerful and occupied – and with much less need of Caroline. She didn't know how to take it. She liked Ginny, and she tried to be glad, but she'd been startled out of her wits – she hadn't seen it coming, though Jeremy assured her she should have done. And, although she knew she was being unreasonable, she found resentment eating into her. She had given up everything for her father – Daniel as well as her career – only to find herself relegated to second place. She felt supplanted.

She tried hard to deny this, reminding herself that she must, surely, be thankful to see her father comfortably established again. Ridiculously, she continued to feel he'd let her down.

Back to where she came in, she reminded herself. They'd urged her at the Central not to make the sacrifice. And now they'd been proved right. So what did she do? Put the clock back? Leave Stonebridge, abandon the practice, apply for a Central post again, and try to pick up her career where she'd put it down eighteen months ago?

Go crawling back to the Central to watch Daniel chasing someone else?

No, she must accept the new life she'd made for herself and remain in Stonebridge, a general practitioner. No good looking back.

But sooner or later, staying in Stonebridge was going to mean marrying Jeremy. As her father wished. Was she ready for that?

The moment of decision overtook her while she was dithering still, and she found she had to make up her mind. For some weeks she'd been half aware that Jeremy seemed to be moving towards a different relationship with her, but even so his proposal took her by surprise.

'You could go on working part-time,' he urged. 'Until we start a family, at any rate.'

Marriage to him would be one solution. It would mean an end to her loneliness. And she had grown amazingly fond of him. He was very companionable, and she liked him so much. The idea of having him to turn to, of sharing her life with someone who cared, and who would always put her first, magnetized her. She'd had more than enough of standing on her own feet. She'd had to do it at the Central when Gavin had gone, and then again in Stonebridge, where after losing her mother she had to watch Daniel too go out of her life. And now even her father no longer needed her. What she longed for was to be part of a family again. And Jeremy would be a good husband, reliable, trustworthy. A splendid partner, just as her father had found him. She opened her mouth to accept. Something stopped her.

'I don't think I'm ready to start raising a family yet,' she said, procrastinating.

Jeremy seemed to think she'd accepted his proposal, though, and that she was merely quibbling the timing of their family. 'Perhaps not,' he agreed cheerfully. 'But that's what I meant. You could go on working in the practice until we were ready to begin raising kids. How would that be?' He looked at her with familiar protective kindness.

If she wanted to be looked after for the rest of her days, she should grab his offer with both hands. Instead she heard herself arguing, evading any commitment.

'No hurry,' he said easily. 'Take your time.' He drove her back to Burvale, and kissed her good night. His arms were amazingly reassuring, and if he'd renewed his urging she'd almost certainly have given in. But he was apparently satisfied with the progress they'd made so far – he opened the door for her, and turned the car.

Caroline waved as he set off down the drive, and then went back towards the house. It was no longer the depressing pile Daniel remembered. Ginny had gone to work on it. The ivy had been stripped, the house, covered in scaffolding, was fast acquiring a new look, as a coat of dark grey Snowcem covered the walls, while the bay windows gleamed white. More scaffolding in the hall, which, up to the dome thirty feet above, was being painted geranium, the plasterwork – detailed and convoluted, bridging walls and ceiling at each level – picked out in brilliant white. There was, Ginny said, to be olive-green carpet on the stairs, whose banisters were already stripped and waxed.

'If you think I'm spoiling it, you must say so at once,' Ginny had said, worrying. Caroline at once assured her she liked the alterations, that the hall had been dismal in the past, but Ginny, carrying a load of anxiety over having usurped Caroline's place, remained uneasy.

Light shone now under the sitting room door – also stripped and waxed – and the strains of a Brahms symphony poured out. Caroline put her head into the room. 'Don't move, either of you. But I'm back – I'm going straight up.'

Ginny jumped to her feet. 'Wouldn't you like a hot drink or something? Can't I get you –'

'No, thanks. I've had a huge meal with Jeremy.'

Her father and Ginny crossed eyes knowingly.

'I'll have an early night now.'

Upstairs in her bedroom, she leaned out of the window and looked across the garden, thinking about Jeremy's proposal. It would be sensible to marry him.

Only he wasn't exactly exciting.

Not like Daniel.

But then that had been a mistake. Those days of hope and magic – had they ever genuinely existed, or had they been little more than the illusions of a dreaming girl? Daniel had wanted to make love to her right enough. No illusion about that. But had that been all? Had the notion of a lifetime together been her own invention? Was it perhaps about time she accepted reality, forgot about dreams and excitement and ecstasy, and settled down here in Stonebridge? Married Jeremy and raised a family? This affection that they shared – an affection that extended to his physical presence, tall and friendly – wasn't this quiet compatibility what marriage should be based on? The garden stretched out before her, pale in the moonlight, and she thought how her mother, who'd loved it, had found her satisfaction in the practice of medicine in Stonebridge. The scent of the tobacco flowers she had planted rose up, reminding Caroline of her childhood here. She could lead the same tranquil existence, she thought, with tea in the garden or a morning stroll among the roses before surgery. With Jeremy by her side, and their children running free in the rolling, heather-covered downland.

The telephone rang.

So much for her early night. At this hour, any call was bound to be for her. She picked up the telephone. 'Dr Milne here.'

'Oh, Doctor, it's Mrs Wakefield.' Caroline's heart sank. Sarah again, out at the caravan site at Edge Side. 'I'm sorry to ring at this time, but I've only just got in, you see, and I don't like the look of Sarah at all.' Just as she'd feared. 'Could you come?'

'On my way. You know what to do in the meantime, though?' Mrs Wakefield knew only too well, of course. She'd had to cope before.

'Oh yes, Doctor, thank you. But I can't get her to respond at all, though. I do feel worried, and if you could –'

'Go straight back and keep on trying. I'll be with you inside ten minutes.' Caroline put the telephone down, pulled on her jeans and an anorak, grabbed her bag and her keys and ran to the garage. As she started the car and drove through the town and out the other side to the escarpment of the downs and Edge Side, she tried to work out, not for the first time, what could be wrong in the Wakefield family. A charming and apparently competent mother – separated from her husband, though, and that must mean something. But what? A sensible, pleasant child, a diabetic, who should be easily controlled – yet who went into coma with calendar-like regularity.

The Edge Side caravan site, apart from the warden

and the Wakefields, was mainly occupied by holiday-makers. The views from it were spectacular – across the weald to the distant blue line of the sea on a clear day – and there was none of the sordid makeshift shanty-town air of Stonebridge's other caravan park between the gas works and the river. To come to Edge Side was a pleasure, had it not been for the fear gnawing away inside Caroline. One day she was going to be too late. One day they were going to lose Sarah.

The caravan was fresh and attractive inside, as usual, neat and organized, flowers in a pottery jug, and Sarah covered, in her bunk, by a bright and cheerful tartan rug.

Mrs Wakefield, slim and red-haired, was white and shaking with anxiety. 'I can't make any impression on her, Doctor. I haven't been able to give her any syrup – I've tried shaking her and smacking her to bring her to, the way you said, so that I could get the syrup down her, but – ' She shook her head. 'She's too far gone.'

Caroline could see that. Sarah was unconscious. Caroline sniffed her breath, nodded, and reached for her bag, after the briefest of examinations. She filled a large syringe with sterile glucose, pulled the blanket down, rolled the sleeve of Sarah's pyjama jacket up, and gave the injection into a vein of her thin little arm.

Sarah, almost certainly, had had her evening insulin, but not her supper, and as a result she had too little sugar in her blood. This was what had caused her to become unconscious – and if the unconsciousness lasted too long, it could lead to brain damage and, finally, to death. This was the anxiety that had been eating Caroline as she drove out to Edge Side.

Mrs Wakefield sighed with relief as the syringe emptied itself into Sarah's bloodstream. 'Thank God you were in when I rang,' she said. 'I don't know what I'd have done if you hadn't been able to get here.'

53

'One of the others would have come. You have all the numbers written down, haven't you?'

'Oh yes, Doctor. I've got them safely in my bag always as well as yours. But it wouldn't be the same. And I – I'd feel such a fool, bothering Dr Armstrong, or Dr Evans.'

This was a general attitude round the practice. All right to call Caroline out in the middle of the night, a slip of a girl and her mother's daughter. But not the senior partners. That would never do, unless you were sure you were dying. 'Any of them would come at once, if you rang, you know,' Caroline said. 'You mustn't hesitate. If one day you do ring and I'm not at home, you mustn't wait for me. You must get straight on to one of the others. You do understand that, don't you?'

'Yes, Doctor, I know. I'm always afraid, though, that one day I won't be able to get anyone. I'll be stuck here alone with her and she'll die, and it'll all be my fault.'

'No need to let your imagination run away with you.' Caroline was crisp. She was sure Mrs Wakefield's fear was genuine, but there were simple measures to be taken. Prevention was, after all, better than cure, and Sarah's coma should have been prevented. One could hardly expect Mrs Wakefield to stay in for ever, but Sarah was only ten and the time now was well after midnight. Surely she was a little young to be left alone in a caravan at this hour, even if she hadn't been diabetic? The signs of the onset of her coma should have been obvious to her mother, if she'd been there, but Mrs Wakefield had distinctly said on the telephone that she'd only just come in, Caroline remembered the words clearly. 'How long had you been out?' she asked.

Mrs Wakefield was flustered. 'Oh, not long, Doctor. Not really. Well, perhaps a bit longer than I meant to be. I just popped down to the Hand & Flower for a drink before closing. For the walk, mainly, it was such a lovely

54

night, and I felt like a drink and a bit of a chat too, you know. Sarah and I had had our tea, and she had her homework to do, and then she wanted to read a chapter of her book – she's a great reader, Sarah – and she was perfectly all right then, so I spoke to Mr Denman – '

'Mr Denman?'

'In the big van. The site warden.'

'Oh yes, I see.'

'I told him I'd be gone for half an hour or an hour – '

And that was wishful thinking, Caroline knew. Half an hour's brisk walking, if she hurried, might just about get Mrs Wakefield to the Hand & Flower. She must have known she'd be away for a minimum of an hour and a half. Probably in fact the period had been more like two hours. Ten until midnight.

No, that didn't work out. The Hand & Flower would close at ten-thirty.

Caroline watched mother and daughter alternately. No point, she decided, in cross-examining Mrs Wakefield now, she'd throw herself into a big cover-up operation. But this was the first discrepancy Caroline had stumbled on during more than a year of looking after Sarah. She'd follow it up when the panic was over. If Mrs Wakefield had no sense of time, if three or four hours were – even occasionally – the same to her as one or two, this could account for Sarah's precarious balance. Poised on a knife edge between her insulin dosage and her food intake, an hour the wrong side could bring disaster – as it had to-night. Tonight they'd caught her in time. She was coming round nicely, and she'd soon be as good as new.

Even so, another hour went by before Caroline felt it was permissible to leave the caravan. By then Sarah had recovered, had a snack, been tucked up again by her mother under the tartan rug, and was sleeping peacefully.

'I'll pop in and see you tomorrow – today, I mean,'

Caroline told Mrs Wakefield as she left. 'Just to make sure Sarah's none the worse. And we'll have a little talk then, see if between us we can get to the bottom of the trouble.'

'Yes, Doctor. Thank you. Thank you ever so much for coming out.'

'Any time. See you some time in the afternoon.'

'Yes, Doctor.'

Caroline drove out of the caravan site, back through the deserted town, and home. She imagined herself to be concentrating on the problem of Sarah and her hypoglycaemic coma, but was surprised to discover, as she put the car away in the garage and walked back into the house through the scented garden, that in fact she was reliving a night at the Central, when she and Daniel had fought to save another child, and had walked back along St Anne's Square together in the dawn.

An enchanted morning, that had been.

5

An Appointment at the Central

The next morning one fact stood out. Clear and inescapable. Daniel was still far too important to her. She had to get him out of her system, and until she did, to attempt to settle down with Jeremy would be fair to neither of them. She'd have to put him off, however disappointed her father might be.

Monday morning, and there weren't too many patients, so surgery finished early. She signed the last prescription form. 'There you are, Mrs Nathan. Get that made up, and take two of the tablets three times a day before meals. Come along and see me again next week, and we'll see how you've been doing.'

'Thank you, Doctor. It's ever so good of you.'

'Only what I'm here for,' Caroline said briskly, clicking her ballpoint pen and beginning to tidy her desk. 'See you next week, then.'

'Yes, Doctor. I'll be here. Thank you.'

Coffee now, and with any luck, as it was early, there might be a chance of talking about Sarah Wakefield to the partners. Caroline stepped along the corridor to the big front room — Dr Armstrong's — where they routinely drank their coffee, settled their lists, and held what amounted to regular case conferences. Today, as they were finalizing their lists, Dr Armstrong enquired if Caroline would do the village clinic at Clandon for him that afternoon.

'Yes, of course,' she said at once. 'That'll be fine. I've

got to go in and see Sarah Wakefield at Edge Side anyway, so I'll be over in that direction.'

'I was rather wondering, as a matter of fact,' Dr Armstrong added, 'if you'd mind taking on Clandon regularly?'

'Oh, I see. Well, I suppose I could.' Caroline was a little put out. The partners had been steadily unloading the scattered village surgeries on to her, at first only occasionally and then, like this, 'I wonder if you'd mind ...' and another outlying village became her responsibility. It wasn't that she minded driving out to the far boundaries of the scattered country practice – if anything, she rather enjoyed it. But the system meant that she had few patients of her own, for whom she undertook continuing care. These village surgeries were held about once a week usually, for the old and infirm, and the mothers and babies, in village halls or a room lent by the vicar, the petrol station or the general store. At Clandon, surgery was held in the front parlour of the house attached to the general store and sub-post office, and Mrs Merriman, the postmistress, provided excellent coffee and home-made cake, as well as acting as unpaid secretarial aide and telephonist. Caroline enjoyed Clandon. But she was becoming more than a little tired of this habit the senior partners had slipped into of using her for most of the outlying chores – the village surgeries were really little more than first-aid posts, and the villagers knew it. Sometimes they even took the bus or the local taxi into Stonebridge and the Hollies, explaining that they'd thought they might be a bit difficult for the young lady out at Mrs Merriman's. Often, Caroline suspected, they looked on her more as the practice nurse than as another doctor.

Dr Evans suggested now that while she was over that way, Caroline might like to look in at Edge Farm, too. The herdsman's wife thought she was expecting again.

'Very well.' Caroline, good resolutions not withstanding, was a trifle snappish. Because this was another chore they tended to dump on her. Obstetrics. The moment anyone became pregnant, no matter whose patient they'd been before, suddenly they were Caroline's. Because she was young, and Peggy Milne's daughter, they looked on her more as a promising young apprentice than as a partner. She sighed. No doubt they'd change in time, and meanwhile she'd have to wear it.

What she was not prepared to wear, though, was Dr Armstrong's next piece of news. He and Dr Evans, he told her, his eyes wary, were taking Dr Peterson into partnership from the first of next month.

'Partnership? Dr Peterson?' Caroline was hardly able to believe her ears. Alan Peterson had come into the practice as a locum, and then as an assistant, after her mother's death, when Caroline had still been at the Central.

Surely she herself had a prior claim to a partnership? And surely they might at least have discussed the question with her, instead of presenting her with a *fait accompli*? Her lips opened in protest – but she closed them firmly a second later. She had to think out her reactions, present her case – if she decided she had one – dispassionately, not deliver an incoherent jumble of emotional protests on the spot. Nearly ten years at the Central had taught her that, as well as a good deal more. So she swallowed the last of her coffee, took her list, and said only, though somewhat curtly. 'From the first of the month? I see. If I'm going to be at Clandon this afternoon I'd better be on my way and get these calls finished before lunch. See you this evening.' Stiff-backed, she left the room. The discussion about Sarah Wakefield would have to wait until this evening. At the moment, she knew, she was too angry to be able to present her anxieties about the child systematically and convincingly. Perhaps, in any case, to see mother and daughter first of all, and try to extract an account of the previous evening's timetable, would be more useful. Closing the door carefully behind her as she weighed up her two conflicting problems – Sarah Wakefield's care, and her own professional future, she left the room.

Two pairs of worried eyes followed her.

'She didn't like it,' Dr Armstrong said flatly.

'I told you she wouldn't.' Dr Evans was unhappy.

'I know you did, but – '

'We should have explained it all to her.'

'How could we?' Dr Armstrong was irritable.

'Of course I know it would have been difficult, but – '

'Out of the question.'

'I suppose so. If only she'd let us know she was engaged – '

'We've been all through this. And as far as we're concerned, as long as she says nothing about her engagement, we simply can't raise it, whatever her father may have told us. And we certainly can't afford to lose Alan, while Caroline dithers about.'

'No. I don't really see what else we could have done, but it seems hard on Caroline, not understanding why.'

'Life is often hard,' Dr Armstrong said sententiously – and, Dr Evans considered, unhelpfully.

'I dare say,' she rejoined sharply. 'But there's no need that I can see for us to make it harder. If you ask me, Caroline's had a raw deal.'

'She'll get over it, I'm sure,' Dr Armstrong rejoined absently, already running his eye down his list.

Outside in her mother's old Rover, Caroline was raging. Unless they had found her inefficient, lazy, unpunctual or unreliable – and she knew very well they had not – she ought to have been considered first for a partnership.

Aside from her family connection with the practice, which she supposed they were entitled to ignore, she was better qualified than Dr Peterson, however likeable he might be.

The *Lancet* was on the car seat beside her, and, almost unconsciously, while her mind ran angrily on, she began flicking through the advertisements. And suddenly, under Paediatrics, the post jumped out of the page at her. The Central were advertising for a senior registrar in her own former department. That must surely be Andrew Marshall's post – he must have been made a consultant at last. At one time, she reminded herself furiously, she'd have been first in line for his job. And then it grabbed her. Why not? That the post should be advertised this week, of all weeks, was a sign she couldn't ignore. A finger pointing the way ahead. She'd show them.

For the remainder of the day, in every spare moment, her thoughts turned to the possibility of going back to the Central. Her visits completed, the Clandon surgery over, Edge Farm, Edge Side and a long talk to Mrs Wakefield and Sarah behind her, she went to Burvale before evening surgery at the Hollies, went up to her room, sat down at her desk and wrote out an application for the post. She unearthed among her papers the photocopies of her curriculum vitae, found she had just enough of them, and caught the post with the lot.

Over a drink after surgery, she explained to Jeremy what she had done. 'I shan't get the post, of course.'

'I don't see why not,' he said encouragingly, though he looked somewhat taken aback. 'You're as likely to get it as anyone, surely? But –'

'No. I'm not. If I'd stayed on at the Central, I'd have as good a chance as anyone. But I've been down here, in general practice, for nearly two years. Out of sight and out of mind. I had to send the application off, though, because – well, for one thing, it seemed so feeble not to, and at least it's a start. It'll remind them that I exist, tell them I'm ready to go back. I'll put in for all the jobs that come up, now, in paediatrics, and I'll begin travelling up and going to lectures and ward rounds, seeing people. Put myself in the picture.'

'You could stay here and we could get married.' But he said it without hope.

Caroline felt a pang of guilt. Only yesterday, he'd asked her to marry him, and he must have been assuming then that she'd be staying here in Stonebridge with him for the rest of her life. And now all she could talk about was the Central, and how to find a job there.

'Oh, Jeremy,' she said contritely. 'It isn't that I want to go away.' Wasn't it, though? Surely that was exactly what it was? 'But I can't stay on for ever in mother's old practice, being the dogsbody.'

'It would do until we married.'

'If we're going to marry' – too late, she saw he'd taken her words as an acceptance of this – 'I'd like a senior post first. Back in London.'

'Before you settle down here to raising a family, you mean?' He was determined to be fair. 'I can understand that, of course. Though I'd much rather you didn't go away at all.'

'I must,' she said. The need was becoming more urgent every second. 'I had a career ahead of me,' she reminded him. 'They all said so. Now I must prove that I still have, even if only to myself.'

'Fair enough. But I shall miss you horribly.'

'We can go on meeting. I shall have weekends off quite often, and you could come up to London sometimes, too – if I ever manage to land a post, that is.'

To her relief, this began to seem far from unlikely. She found herself short-listed. She had been, in fact, too humble in her expectations, without realizing it had been a good deal undermined at Stonebridge in her opinion of herself. To be treated, both at home and in the practice, as a well-intentioned juvenile had made her begin to doubt her capabilities. If only she had been able to watch the reception of her application at the Central she would have been reassured.

The administration did the first sifting of applicants, and at this stage Caroline was put straight on to a preliminary short list, to be looked over by Sir Graham Williamson and Dr Walter Berkeley. Both these pundits received a considerable shock when, along with Daniel Harcourt's application, which they were expecting, they saw Caroline's.

Until then, both of them had been regarding Daniel's appointment as more or less settled. But as soon as he saw Caroline's name, Sir Graham jumped to a false conclusion. Daniel, he thought, was not only his own registrar, but another Mortimer's man. Walter Berkeley had whistled up Caroline in an attempt to ensure that someone trained at the Central, instead of an infiltrator from Mortimer's, was given the senior registrar's post.

'Caroline Milne thinking of returning to us, is she?' he enquired.

'First I've heard of it,' Dr Berkeley said testily. But his brain was working fast, the advantages that Sir Graham envisaged racing across his mind. He was irritated, however, with Caroline. She'd paid not the remotest attention to his advice when she'd been so set on going into general practice, and now, when, inevitably, she discovered he'd been right, she hadn't the common courtesy to inform him. He'd half a mind not to back her.

Sir Graham was highly suspicious. 'Didn't you know?'

'Not a thing.' Wily Walter was limpid-eyed, but then he often was.

Sir Graham scrutinized him dubiously.

'Truly,' Walter Berkeley added with a glint, having met no problem in interpreting his director's expression.

'What are we going to do, then? Two exceptional candidates, we've got now. One of them Central-trained,' he added craftily, hoping to entice Dr Berkeley into committing himself to an anti-Mortimer's stand.

Walter Berkeley, though, saw the trap. 'True,' he agreed serenely. 'But a woman, after all. Dr Milne might well find it more difficult to handle the men – in a considerable majority here – than Dr Harcourt would. A woman who doesn't know her own mind, too,' he threw in disgustedly. This was an impromptu offering, but he saw at once that it had foxed Sir Graham, now uncertain which way his assistant director was facing. Deviously, he emphasized the point. 'Two years ago she was set on leaving the Central and spending her days in general practice,' he complained. 'Now, suddenly, without a word to either of us – a gross discourtesy, if you ask me – out of the blue, she puts in for this post. What's behind it? We don't know. Is it a whim? Will she ever present herself for interview? Or will she have another change of mind by then?'

Sir Graham thought this response a little unfair of Dr Berkeley, and said so. At this stage Wily Walter, that unparalleled operator, broke off the discussion.

On the day of the interview Caroline, never for a moment imagining she might already be a favourite for the post, woke early, and in a state of jitters. Perhaps it had all been a mistake. They probably hadn't meant to short-list her at all. When she arrived, they'd be politely noncomprehending, wondering why she'd appeared. Or she'd sit in the waiting room, never being called for interview, and finally trail ingloriously home, having seen no one.

Her stomach was an empty ache.

She went down to breakfast, poured a cup of tea, refused, shuddering, the bacon and egg Ginny offered, and spread her toast with nervous fingers. The telephone rang, and she jumped a mile, spilt her tea. Ridiculous. Normally the telephone rang half a dozen times during breakfast, and she dealt with the calls easily.

'I'll answer,' Ginny said quickly. She spoke crisply to the caller, gave Dr Peterson's number.

A car appeared in the drive. Jeremy's Triumph. Caroline went to the front door.

'Just looked in to wish you luck,' he said.

'Thanks, I need it. I'm in a flat spin.'

'All interviews are hell,' he said easily. 'But you'll be fine once you get there, I'm sure.'

'I expect I shall,' she admitted. 'I'm usually OK once it starts.'

He patted her encouragingly. 'That's my girl. When are you leaving? Can I give you a lift or anything?'

'I thought I ought to get the ten to nine, to be on the safe side.'

'Better come now, with me, and I'll run you to the station before I go to the office.'

'Oh, would you?'

'No trouble. You look super, you know.' His eyes told her he meant this. 'That colour suits you no end – you should wear it more often. Rust, is it?'

'They call it terracotta.'

'It does something for you. You'll knock them all for six, I shouldn't wonder.'

Caroline was already feeling better. And Jeremy not only drove her to the station, but went on to the platform with her, bought her an armful of magazines and a box of chocolates, told her again how smashing she looked, saw her into the carriage and shut the door on her tenderly, wished her good luck again – 'not that you need it, you'll do OK, they'll take one look at you and invite you on to the staff' – and said if she rang him from Waterloo that evening he'd meet her when she returned.

The train drew out, and he stood waving cheerily on the platform, while Caroline sank back in her seat feeling cherished, beautiful, secure.

As the train drew nearer to London, though, these morale-boosting sensations dissipated, and she found herself fighting panic again, and asking herself why in the world she had insisted on applying for a senior post in London when she could have married Jeremy. She could have been sitting comfortably at home planning her wedding, instead of sitting in this train sick with dread.

Or could she? Wasn't that a bit tame?

She could try pulling herself together. She didn't, after all, expect to land the job, only to remind the Central of her existence. So why sit like this in the taxi, shaking like an advanced case of Parkinson's?

As soon as she climbed the steps of the main entrance, her confidence came surging back. This was the Central, where she belonged. She had come home. Even to tread the familiar corridors was invigorating. And unexpectedly, without warning, flashed the glimmer of hope that refused to be suppressed. In the Central she might run across Daniel again.

She did run across him, of course. Sitting in the waiting room, ready to be interviewed, like herself, for the post of senior registrar to the department of child health.

6

An Engagement

The meeting clearly shook Daniel. Neither his own chief
nor Dr Berkeley had thought of informing him of the
opposition. Undecided whom to support, they'd kept their
mouths shut around the department, and he – like a fool,
he now realized – had supposed this to mean that they
hadn't wished to be seen to be taking his own appointment
as a foregone conclusion.

'I didn't know you were putting in for the post,' he
snapped accusingly at Caroline, eyeing her, she decided,
as if she'd that minute crawled out from behind the
panelling and he was reaching for the aerosol can. 'I
thought you'd retired into country life for the remainder
of your days.' His voice was cutting, his eyes were stony.
That they might conceal shock and an aching wound
never occurred to her.

'My father has remarried,' she said briefly. 'So I'm free
to work in London again.'

He looked astonished, but before he had a chance to
reply, he was called for interview. He left the room,
squaring his shoulders in a manner Caroline discovered
she had never forgotten.

However, she did her best to forget it, making polite
conversation to the two remaining occupants of the waiting room, a Scotsman and a Pakistani, while she told
herself that the appointment had obviously been ear-
marked for Daniel, the interviews no more than a
formality. The Scot and the Pakistani agreed with her.

Her name was called.

In the board room, behind the table, she found four people – Sir Graham Williamson and Dr Walter Berkeley from the department, with the dean of the medical school and the house governor.

'Well, Dr Milne, have a chair. Nice to see you again.' Sir Graham opened the batting with what turned out to be misleading geniality, though it lulled Caroline moment-arily into supposing they might be as glad to see her as she was to see them. In fact, she was taken by surprise by the uprush of emotion that seized her as she confronted them, and the delight she experienced at being with them was, unknown to her, mirrored in her face, while her first words, 'It's lovely to be here', were so plainly genuine that Walter Berkeley, who'd been teetering on the brink of doing Sir Graham a favour by appointing Daniel – a favour for which, naturally, he'd expect a *quid pro quo* – was won over. He decided he'd land this appointment for Caroline Milne if he had to keep them sitting here all night.

No one, though, would have guessed it. He interviewed her harshly. So stringent was he, in fact, that both the dean and the house governor were taken in, concluding that Walter had never forgiven his formerly favourite registrar for abandoning him nearly two years ago, and was set on seeing her pay the price, here and now. They rallied to her defence, and fed her with the answers to his more difficult questions.

Sir Graham, while maintaining a chairman's imparti-ality, was equally deceived, imagining Dr Berkeley to be nursing a grudge – a habit of his. And then, didn't they say, of the Central, once you put a foot wrong there, you were out, and you'd never get back? At Mortimer's those days were over, had been for years, but the Central was an old-fashioned place, notorious for refusing to move with the times. Sir Graham had originally wanted the post for Daniel, but Walter Berkeley's onslaught on Caroline upset him. Walter really shouldn't bully her like that. She was a good girl, hardworking and clever, and he was being grossly unfair to her, simply because she'd put her duty to her father before her responsibility to Walter. A gentle and charming creature, Caroline Milne, Sir Graham decided, as well as able and conscientious, and he wouldn't be at all sorry to see her appointed. He'd enjoy working with her.

Caroline herself was not, as it happened, as upset by Walter Berkeley's treatment as these gullible males imagined. For one thing, she had always been good at interviews, keeping her head and providing clear straight answers. And then, she was about the only individual in the room not taken in by Wily Walter. Not for nothing had she been first his house physician and then his registrar. She recognized his technique, and while she had no inkling of the full enormity of his behaviour, she was reasonably sure he was engaged in putting her through her paces. The cross-examination came to an end with what, to Dr Berkeley, remained the crux of the matter. Caroline had already admitted that she had been mistaken in supposing general practice to be the right line for her. She was indeed, as they had told her two years ago, better suited to hospital medicine, and while she was far from regretting the additional experience – especially with children in their own homes – she had gained during this period in Stonebridge, she intended to return to hospital medicine permanently, either at the Central, or, failing that, wherever else they wanted her.

'How do we know you won't change your mind again?' Walter was waspish, and the three men at the table with him hated him for it. 'Career off back to wherever it is, to this practice of yours, and tell us you've got to look after your father?'

'My father has remarried, I'm glad to say. And the practice have appointed a junior partner already in my mother's place.'

Dr Berkeley subsided. 'Thank you, Dr Milne.'

Sir Graham glanced along the table. 'Any further questions? Dean? Mr Ward? No? Thank you, Dr Milne. If you'd be good enough to wait in the adjoining room, we'll let you know.

'Thank you, sir.'

The house governor rose with alacrity, opened the door and ushered her out – a courtesy he failed to extend to any of the other candidates. In the waiting room, Caroline rejoined Daniel and the Scotsman, the Pakistani being called in as she returned. Conversation was even more strained than it had been earlier, and the tension was in no way eased when the Pakistani, Dr Shah, came back and the Scot, Dr Tomlinson, went in. Daniel remarked that they had been taken in strict alphabetical order, Dr Shah agreed and asked Caroline if she had travelled far. About two hundred miles, she told him, from Stonebridge – near Broomhurst. Did he know it? He did not. Where had he come from? Bradford. At this point Daniel brilliantly enquired if it was colder there than in London, and Dr Shah replied that it was, but that the central heating in the hospital was excellent. About the only thing, he added morosely, that functioned adequately. Daniel, who was clearly determined to keep the conversation alive at all costs while not addressing a word to Caroline – whose eye he had successfully avoided since her return to the room, although they sat facing one another – asked how many beds the hospital had. Dr Shah told him, and enquired about the number at the Central. At this juncture Dr Tomlinson rejoined them, followed by the house governor's secretary, who asked if they'd care for a cup of tea while they were waiting. Caroline said a cup of tea would be very nice, thank you so much, and the other three echoed her.

In the board room they already had their tea. They had also eliminated Dr Shah and Dr Tomlinson, and were discussing the rival merits of Caroline and Daniel.

'I don't know that we necessarily want a girl running the department,' Wily Walter probed.

'Male chauvinist,' the dean replied, without heat. 'I think it would be very nice for you all.'

'Hear, hear.' Sir Graham, to everyone's stupefaction, endorsed this. Before they had fully recovered, he confounded them further. 'I don't know,' he confided, 'that it would be altogether advantageous to have two Mortimer's men at the helm, so to speak, of the department of child health at the Central. What do you think?' He beamed benignly up and down the table.

Since everyone but Sir Graham himself had been repeating this exact opinion monotonously for the past three months, three jaws dropped with almost audible clicks. This was the moment, too, when Wily Walter knew he'd landed the post for Caroline, but he continued to tread warily. 'Did you gain the impression that Dr Milne was serious in her intention to return permanently to hospital medicine?' he enquired dubiously.

Three voices assured him they had seldom been more certain of anything, and the dean, who had been on Caroline's side from the outset – he liked to see posts go to his own students – remarked that it would be a pity to allow her to escape a second time. The hospital could ill-afford to lose young physicians of her calibre.

Caroline was in.

And Daniel, it followed, was out.

'A little hard on Harcourt, who must have been expecting to be appointed,' Dr Berkeley commented craftily.

'No right to jump to conclusions like that.' The house governor was sharp.

'He certainly had no sort of intimation from me that he could take anything for granted.' Sir Graham was even sharper.

'All the same,' Dr Berkeley persevered. 'It would be natural if he had assumed –'

'Must expect to meet disappointments like this occasionally.' The dean was blithe. 'All in the day's work. No doubt he'll weather it. Sensible young man, so I'm told.' Lean, red-faced and balding, he was a tough man himself, and demanded fortitude and endurance from all around him, including his unfortunate patients.

'Very foolish if he permitted himself to count on the appointment,' Sir Graham added thinly. 'Shall we have Dr Milne back now? Are we ready for her?'

'I'll fetch her,' the house governor said enthusiastically. 'And get my secretary to get rid of the others.' He stuck his head in the door of his own office, gave terse instructions, and then walked cheerfully along the corridor to the waiting room. Four pairs of anguished eyes met his. 'Dr Milne, if you would spare us a few minutes more,' he said, and bore her away. 'They're going to offer it to you,' he told her, and took her back into the board room, settling her into her chair as if she might break.

Sir Graham formally offered her the post.

Dazed, Caroline accepted it.

Sir Graham told her how glad he was she'd be working among them again, the dean thought she'd make a wise decision while Walter Berkeley, visibly unmasking, trusted she'd learnt something useful from her period in general practice, he dared to say she might well have done, but he was relieved to learn she was back where she belonged. Or would be, six weeks from now.

The party broke up. Walter Berkeley consulted his watch, announced he still had a minute or two to spare, and Caroline had better be thinking about her accommodation. 'Get it organized today, while you're in town.'

Caroline, still slightly stunned, said faintly that he mustn't bother, she could easily arrange something by correspondence. Or over the telephone, if it came to that.

'No need.' Walter was in holiday mood now. He'd appointed his candidate, and now he was going to look after her, see her properly established. 'Andrew Marshall wants to get rid of his flat. You'd better have it. Should do you nicely. Come along, we'll go and see him.' He set off at his usual fast trot, Caroline loping behind him in a manner very familiar to her. But Andrew had left outpatients, where he'd been taking Walter's clinic. Sister thought he'd popped back to his flat for a cup of tea.

'Ah,' Dr Berkeley twinkled at her. 'Had mine in the board room. About the only advantage of these selection committees they keep wanting me to sit on. They do see to it you get a cup of tea on time. You'll remember Dr Milne, Sister.' Since Sister turned out to be Prue Macfarlane, the staggering blonde staff nurse from Casualty, they recognized one another at once. 'Glad to say Dr Milne's rejoining us. Taking over Dr Marshall's post when he goes down to Sussex.'

Prue looked staggered, and then, though she quickly hid it, upset and worried. Caroline saw at once that the entire hospital had assumed Daniel would be appointed, and that Prue had more than a passing interest in the decision. So that was who Daniel was going around with now.

'Well, I'll be off home too,' Dr Berkeley announced. 'Got another of those damned committees at 6.30, though. Tell you what, you come along with me, my dear, and we'll drop in on Andrew on the way.'

73

Andrew, who opened the door of his flat himself, was unmistakably astonished to discover Wily Walter and Caroline standing there awaiting him. He sagged slightly, and was pulling himself together just as Dr Berkeley informed him of Caroline's appointment, when his usual composure totally deserted him.

Walter Berkeley, by now more than a little bored with Caroline's accommodation problem, took off while Andrew was still scrambling for words. 'Take her in and show her your flat,' he adjured him. 'That's why I brought her along. She's going to need one, so it seems to me she'd better take over yours.' He patted Caroline. 'Look forward to seeing you on the first,' he said. 'Not next month, no, but the one after. Now get yourself a flat here, and you're all set. That's right.' He nodded to himself, and raced off downstairs.

Andrew gulped. 'Er – yes – well, I – Caroline, it's great to see you, and I'm delighted to know – come in, come in. Um – well, the fact is, I don't exactly know, but – er – we – '

Caroline thought she had better cut through this. 'Have you already let your flat?' she asked. 'Because I don't actually have to – it was Dr Berkeley's idea, you see, not mine at all, and I can easily – '

'Trouble is, in a way I have let it. I'd more or less arranged for Daniel to have it. But then, you see, we thought he was going to – ' Hastily he abandoned this line. 'I can't very well dispose of it without finding out if he still – I don't know if he – '

'If Daniel is having it, I can easily look for somewhere else.'

'Well, yes, but the thing is, I dare say he doesn't – tell you what, let's give him a ring, shall we? If he wants this flat, he's got one of his own to dispose of, in any case. So perhaps you could have his?' This thought obviously cheered Andrew considerably, and he went briskly to the telephone, rang Daniel, and informed him that Caroline was looking for a flat. 'Wily Walter brought her along here to look at mine, but I've explained to her that you're taking it over, and I've suggested she comes over to look at yours? OK?'

Presumably Daniel must have agreed, for Andrew, after only a brief pause, said, 'Good. I'll tell her – she'll be on her way stat.' He turned to Caroline. 'He's expecting you.'

There seemed to be no alternative but to thank Andrew and go, and Caroline, her mind whirling, hardly knowing whether she was glad or sorry about it, arrived on Daniel's doorstep and began talking as incoherently as Andrew had done a few minutes back. 'I'm sorry, Daniel, I really had no intention of bothering you, but Andrew insisted it was all right, and so I – well, I thought I'd better come straight over, but don't for a minute imagine I expect you to – I mean, if you've promised anyone, or you – after all, I –'

'Do you want it or don't you?'

'I'm dreadfully sorry, I didn't mean –'

'Don't you want the place, then?' His brusqueness, that she took for anger at her temerity, in fact covered a secret certainty that Andrew had boobed, that his own squalid pad was never going to suit the girl from Burvale. If he'd had a bit of warning he would at least have been able to do a spot of tidying up, but even so . . .

'Oh yes, it would be marvellous if I could have it. But you mustn't feel you –'

She was lying to him. Out of sheer bloody politeness, she was lying to him. That was how far apart they were. And now he'd have to show her the flat. He galloped her through it, monosyllabic, throwing room and cupboard doors open with a crash and shutting them with a slam.

Caroline had never, in her daydreams over the past two, long, lonely years, seen their next meeting like this – they might have been two antagonistic estate agents going through a property. And then the flat, untidy and bookish as it was, brought back disturbing memories. It told her something about Daniel, too, that she would have preferred to have forgotten.

She took the flat, and was thankful, as soon as the routine details were settled – of the handover of the flat at the end of the following month, when Andrew would be leaving the Central for his new consultant post, and vacating his own flat – to escape. Before she left Daniel congratulated her stiffly on gaining the job, and she heard herself twittering falsely back, as he went downstairs with her to the street entrance. Seeing a cruising taxi, she hailed it, panic-stricken, and was borne off – not daring to glance back – to Waterloo, where she rang Jeremy.

He answered the telephone at once. 'How did it go?' he asked, and she could tell he was cautious, ready to condole with her.

'I got it.'

'You did? Great. That's my girl. We'll have us a celebration, shall we? Or will you be too exhausted?'

'No, no,' she assured him eagerly. 'I'm not tired. I'd love to celebrate.' And to hell with you and all my pathetic girlish dreams, Daniel Harcourt. Get lost.

Only, of course, he wasn't going to get lost. In six weeks they'd be working together, and how was she going to hold the new job down with Daniel glowering away in the background, day in, day out, junior to her and resenting it every step of the way?

Perhaps, though, as he hadn't been given the senior post, he'd put in for something else – go back to

Mortimer's, say. And she'd be free of him. This thought failed lamentably to restore her spirits.

Jeremy, however, achieved this very nicely.

Waiting for her at the station, though she didn't know it, he'd been on edge, in almost as much of a turmoil about her and her new post as she was in about Daniel. He'd begun taking her out for reasons that had started by being mixed, and had stayed that way. He'd always liked her and admired her, but he'd found her slightly alarming, too. She was so brilliant. But his motives had not been, at that time, entirely straightforward. He'd not been unaware of the fact it would do him no harm to go around with his senior partner's only child. As their companionship had developed, though, and he'd begun to know Caroline, he'd forgotten his strategy, and looked forward to his evenings with her as to nothing else in his week. Almost without noticing how it came about, he contemplated marrying her and settling down.

He didn't, to be honest, see anything standing in his way – Caroline was meeting no one else, she was only, her father had told him more than once (wishful thinking, but he hadn't realized this) filling in time in the practice, so he hadn't been in any hurry – more fool him, he thought bitterly – until Robert's wedding to Ginny. That occasion had shaken him to the core. Suddenly, standing in the parish church at Stonebridge, he'd been overwhelmed by an intense longing to walk down that same aisle with Caroline on his arm. His wife.

So he'd proposed, and she'd put him off. But he hadn't been worried. He'd imagined they had all the time in the world ahead of them, and she'd come round to it. After all, why not? What else was she likely to have in mind? He wasn't going to run after her. He'd simply sit and wait, and she'd be his. So he'd thought.

But now she was going back to London to work. He

didn't know what to do, but again this evening, waiting for her at the station in his car, he surprised himself. He was glad she'd made her decision. By now he knew her well enough to understand that she was doing the right thing for herself. He'd have to take her on her own terms. And so, there in the station car park, he was genuinely thankful she'd pulled it off, had, against all his expectations, landed the post. He wanted to give her a celebration to set the seal on her achievement. She was in the mainstream again, swimming strongly, her career ahead of her. But what was he going to do himself? His own career, until now, had given him no anxiety. He liked Stonebridge, he enjoyed his work, he'd seen himself as established there, settling down with Caroline, eventually taking over the partnership when her father retired.

What now?

Was he going to throw all this away and follow Caroline to London, like some camp-follower? His pride rebelled, but his love for Caroline at least posed the question.

She arrived off the London train, and he hugged her joyfully. 'Congratulations.' He kissed her. 'Well done. You look super in that suit. I bet you knocked them all.'

Caroline recollected. 'You know, I believe I may have done, a bit.'

'More than a bit, I'd say. When do you start?'

'In six weeks.'

'Quite soon,' he said blankly. Hastily he pulled himself together. 'I thought we'd have a real celebration tonight, go to the Mitre and do ourselves proud, eh?'

'Super.'

A fantastic evening. A perfect end to a wonderful day, Caroline decided, perhaps helped by the fact that she was both starving and excited, more than ready to do justice to the Mitre's food and drink.

The excitement and exhaustion combined to make her more beautiful than Jeremy had ever known her. Caroline glowed, the Mitre, determinedly Tudor, all dark polished oak, mullioned windows, wrought-iron lanterns, glowed back and brought her its best. And its best, as Jeremy had discovered when he'd taken clients there for lunch, was very good indeed.

Over coffee and brandy before a great log fire in the red leather lounge, he proposed again, producing a ring, a solitaire diamond that astonished Caroline, and that he'd had in stock since the evening she'd turned him down, he told her. This evening she accepted without reservation. Without his support and reassurance, today would have been nothing. With him, though, it had been triumphant. She needed him. He was her life's partner.

'I may have to follow you to London,' Jeremy announced, jokingly. Neither of them knew if he meant it.

7

Case Conference

As soon as she came into coffee, they spotted her ring.

'Caroline has some news for us, I see,' Dr Evans remarked coyly.

For a second or two Caroline, who supposed them to be referring to her new post, was at a loss to account for the jokey atmosphere.

'May I enquire who is to be the lucky man?' Alan Peterson asked – he often used these stereotyped phrases, and in an embittered moment Caroline had told herself that it must be this that gave him his advantage over her, that had won him the partnership.

'Would I be out of order in suggesting his name may begin with a J?' Marjorie Evans demanded, raising untidy brows over twinkling brown eyes. She was in fact amazingly relieved to find that the rumour about Caroline's impending engagement was correct, and they had not passed her over mistakenly.

Caroline, though, wanted to throw things. 'Yes.' She was curt. 'Jeremy Watson. Quite right. And I got the post at the Central.' She hurled the information furiously in their direction before turning aside to look through the day book for her visits.

This stopped them in their tracks.

'You got – ?' Dr Evans's mouth hung open, and the brown eyes went blank with shock.

'You – you've got – they gave you – they *appointed*

you to that post? The one you – the one that was advertised?' Plainly Dr Armstrong didn't really believe her.

'Senior registrar at the Central?' Dr Peterson filled in the gaps, as a reliable junior partner should. 'You've actually been appointed, Caroline?'

'That's right.' She was abrupt.

'Wow.' Dr Peterson gazed at her with respect. 'Congratulations indeed. See what we've been entertaining unawares?' He beamed.

Unawares was dead accurate, Caroline told herself.

'A whizz-kid, no less,' Dr Peterson continued happily, unmistakably delighted.

'I am so glad, my dear.' Marjorie Evans recovered her voice. 'Your mother would have been so proud.'

'Indeed she would.' Dr Armstrong, too, pulled himself together. 'When do you take it up?'

'In six weeks. I hope that'll be all right.'

'Have to be. Can't stand in your way, can we? Not over an appointment like this.'

'I suppose this boyfriend of yours thought he'd better get the ring safely on your finger before those loose-living types at the Central have a chance to work on you?' Alan Peterson commented, with a broad grin.

Caroline stared. A new idea, this. But probably correct, she saw. Could it be that Jeremy was afraid he might lose her?

As she went back to the Hollies after lunch for the weekly case conference, she encountered Alan again. They made their way through the hall to the lobby where they left their coats.

'Who are we supposed to be discussing this afternoon?' he asked.

'My diabetic child, Sarah Wakefield, for one,' Caroline said. 'I wish I could make the senior partner take that family seriously. I'm sure there must be something in the

81

background that we know nothing about, some funny situation that's been playing havoc with the child, and that I haven't so far been able to track down. So do back me up, if you can. I'd like to have a discussion in depth about the family, and not be brushed off as alarmist, as he did last time I raised them. I've only got the child as a patient, you see, he's got mum, and so – '

'No, he hasn't. He gave her to me, a week or two back.'

'Oh, for God's sake,' Caroline exploded. 'If he was going to get rid of her, why couldn't he have given her to me? He positively revels in splitting up families, I sometimes think.'

'I'm a bit puzzled about her, as a matter of fact, so I'll gladly join you.'

'I thought,' Dr Armstrong began, when Caroline brought up Sarah Wakefield, 'that we'd settled that she was to go for a consultant opinion in London?'

'That's right,' Caroline said. 'And that's another point. I made an appointment for her to see my old chief at the Central. But she didn't keep it.'

'Didn't keep it?'

'No. So when they told me she hadn't turned up, I went out to the caravan site and saw Mrs Wakefield. She said she'd overslept that morning, and when she woke it was too late to get to the hospital on time.'

'Silly woman. I suppose you made another appointment?'

'Oh yes, I did. But it's two months to wait.'

'You'd better go out and see the mother the day before and read her the riot act about being on time in the morning.'

'Oh, I will. But – '

'In the meantime I don't see what we can do. Discuss it again after we have the consultant's report, eh?' He glanced down at his notebook. 'Now, old Mr – '

'I am a little unhappy about the present set-up, as far as the Wakefields are concerned. I don't feel we can quite – '

'In a better position to judge once the consultant has seen her.'

'Yes, but – '

'I'm a bit uneasy about Mrs Wakefield, as it happens,' Alan Peterson weighed in. 'You remember you asked me to take her over?'

'Sure.'

'She came up for a repeat prescription – she seems to me to be on rather a high dosage of meprobamate, but I gave it to her, as it was the first time I'd seen her, and she's been on it for years. I'm wondering, though, if perhaps it might not be a good plan to try reducing it?' He spoke cautiously, for he knew he was in effect querying his senior partner's treatment.

'What's she on now?'

Alan consulted the medical record in his hand, and read out the dosage.

'Far too high, of course. Afraid I missed that. Glad you picked it up. Very sensible of you, Alan.'

'She never told me she was on a tranquillizer.' Caroline was irritable – more, in fact, with Dr Armstrong for not giving her the full picture than with Mrs Wakefield. 'But if she was doped to the eyeballs, it does explain why she overslept on the morning of Sarah's appointment. It might also be part of the explanation for Sarah going into coma. Suppose Mrs Wakefield's a bit vague, and there's no routine in that caravan, how can the poor child be expected to balance her food intake and her insulin? We may be on to something there.'

'The trouble is, Mrs Wakefield was one of your mother's patients, Caroline, and none of us know, except from the notes, very much about her. And as far as I recollect, there's not much down in the notes – your mother wasn't in the habit of committing details to paper – it's led to a number of problems, as you must have seen for yourself by now. What have you actually got down there, Alan?'

'The first note after she moved here simply says "marital breakdown, now living with daughter in caravan at Edge Side. Rep. Mist." And before that it's a series of Rep. Mist., right back to the original prescription, where it simply says, "Depressed. Too much housework and hates London", with an exclamation mark. Before that there are details about her pregnancy.'

'Not very helpful, altogether. But I'm glad you raised the case, Caroline. It's a good deal more worrying than I'd grasped. We'll have to keep an eye on the pair of them, Sarah and her mother. It's a bit dicey, I must say, a diabetic child plus a mother on tranquillizers, after a broken marriage, living alone in a caravan well outside the town.'

'Thoroughly unsatisfactory, if you ask me.' Marjorie Evans was downright. 'I've never seen either of them, though. Perhaps you or Alan could pop in, Caroline, and give Mrs Wakefield a pep talk about being on time with Sarah's meals and so on, and generally cast an eye around the place.'

'I'll do that,' Caroline promised.

'Before you leave us for fresh woods and pastures new,' Dr Evans added, the twinkle back in her eye. 'Tell me, Caroline, how is that young man of yours taking the postponement of the wedding while you go gallivanting off to the Central for a year or two? Or are you going to marry before you take up the post?'

'No, I shall take up the job first.' Caroline was brusque, though she reminded herself hastily that Dr Evans had, after all, brought her into the world and had a right to be interested in what she was doing with her life.

'Must be a bit of a blow to him,' Dr Armstrong said. 'After all, from what your father told us, we expected you to be married before Christmas. But perhaps he was jumping the gun a bit?'

A bit? Talk about going off at half-cock, Caroline thought furiously. What on earth could her father have said? 'There was never any question of marrying before Christmas,' she said shortly.

When she reached home that evening after surgery she was ready to challenge him. However, she found Jeremy there before her, with champagne on ice, and a celebration meal in the process of being organized, so she had to swallow her irritation.

'You look a bit fussed,' Jeremy told her. 'What's bothering you? The new job?'

'No, the old one. But it doesn't matter any more.'

'Forget everything and everyone except me,' he suggested.

As if that would ever be possible, Caroline thought regretfully.

'And go and change into something fantastic.'

'Of course I will,' she said, and kissed him. 'Lovely to come back and find you here.'

'I love you,' he told her.

'And I love you,' she promised. 'I'll go and change.'

In her room she hunted through her cupboard. She seemed to possess little that could by any stretch of the imagination be described as fantastic – apart from a few tweed skirts and pullovers purchased locally, her clothes remained those she'd owned two years or more ago in London, and they'd never, even then, been notable as trend-setters. In Stonebridge she'd gone cheerfully to medical sherry parties and dinners in one of her two long skirts – a printed cotton and a patterned velvet. But Jeremy, she was sure, did not have either of them in mind when he spoke of something fantastic. He'd bought champagne, his eyes were bright with – with what? Triumph. That was it. He intended tonight to be an evening to remember, and he wouldn't thank her for appearing in her old skirt with one of her familiar tops.

There remained only that drift of chiffon in beige and white that she'd worn to the Central ball with Daniel, and she could hardly climb into that for a little family dinner.

Why not?

Very likely both Jeremy and her father would be pleased. She knew she looked – yes, exactly what Jeremy had demanded – fantastic in it. But it wasn't Jeremy's dress. It carried memories of the Central and Daniel, of that dawn when they'd walked together through the quiet London squares, when the air smelt fresh and newly washed, and the world had been young around them, filled with promise. Daniel, lean and gangling, briefly tidied into his velvet jacket and a gleaming shirt, had walked by her side, talking, she remembered vividly, mainly about the child whose leukaemia they'd just diagnosed. But he'd held her hand as they rushed through the squares and over the bridge towards Waterloo, and she'd been certain, then, that they were in love for ever. But it had all been a mistake. She knew that now. First Gavin and then Daniel. She had looked for a lifetime's loving, when neither of them had seen more than a passing affair.

She twisted Jeremy's ring on her finger, and took herself in hand. She loved Jeremy. Not in the exact way she'd loved Daniel, but in a far more sensible way. They'd make a good partnership. She'd work at it.

And she'd begin now, this minute, by wearing Daniel's dress.

She came down the wide staircase – all scaffolding gone

at last, olive carpet laid, shining coral walls and the great chandelier glittering under the high arching skylight – and Jeremy caught his breath.

'I've never seen you in that before,' he said. 'You look terrific.' He kissed her, took her into his arms the instant she arrived at the foot of the stairs and held her close, with desire riding him, so that she couldn't fail to be affected by the power of his own excitement. The evening began to make sense, and she forgot her misgivings and the trace of guilt that had been stealthily creeping into her dealings with him.

'Hey, look at you. Fabulous.' Ginny passed them with a huge platter of stuffed eggs, smoked salmon in rolls and mounds of shrimps in pink mayonnaise. 'Take this and put it on the table for me, and I'll go and *do* something to myself.'

Her father came into the hall from the sitting room, and stared as though he'd never seen her before. 'Caroline,' he said, and stared some more. 'You are looking extraordinarily beautiful, my dear.'

In spite of her earlier annoyance with him, Caroline was swept by an uprush of affection, and went swiftly across to him and kissed him. After all, he'd been right, hadn't he? Perhaps he had simply seen farther ahead than she had herself. 'I'm so happy, Dad,' she told him. 'That's what does it.'

But suddenly as she spoke she knew it was a lie. Excitement and champagne, and being fussed over, were making her beautiful tonight. Not happiness.

Her father believed her, though. 'It makes me happy too,' he said, delighted, 'to see you and Jeremy together, both of you part of my family. Your health.' He took the glass Jeremy offered and raised it. 'Caroline and Jeremy, many, many happy years,' he said confidently. They all drank. Caroline felt a fraud. Hastily she told herself not to be silly. Probably she was over-tired. That must be the trouble. A hard day yesterday, too many late calls for weeks before that, and then today the case conference, a number of difficult visits, followed by a packed and arduous evening surgery. She'd been up and working since seven, and now – she glanced at the old grandfather clock, ticking away solidly in the alcove to which Ginny had consigned him – now it was nine in the evening. She sipped her champagne, willing herself to regain the joy she'd known only minutes earlier, when Jeremy had held her. Everything had been all right then. Everything was going to be all right again. It had to be.

Her father went upstairs, and reappeared, carrying the slim velvet case that held, Caroline knew, her mother's pearls. He stopped at the foot of the stairs, opened it. 'Peggy would want you to have these,' he said. He took out the heavy rope. 'Come here, and let me put them on for you.'

Caroline stepped obediently across the hall, and bent her neck. Her father's hands fumbled in her hair. 'Your hair is much longer than your mother's,' he grumbled, fiddling. Finally the pearls were fastened, and he turned her about, looked her up and down. 'That's it,' he said, pleased. 'They suit you. My engagement present to you – from me and Peggy, my dear.' He kissed her almost sadly, and Caroline clung to him, praying fervently that Ginny would not choose that moment to make her appearance.

Meanwhile Jeremy, who had been looking on with considerable approval, added his voice. 'You look wonderful in them, Caroline. Absolutely terrific. You look pretty marvellous, anyway, tonight. I'm beginning to suspect being engaged is good for you.'

'Of course it is,' Caroline agreed enthusiastically, in the voice she might have used to encourage a child patient who'd just swallowed some nasty medicine. Again

88

she felt a fraud. This was meaningless banter. She couldn't keep it up for the rest of her days. Surely she and Jeremy could not truly be as out of touch as this?

He put a hand up, felt the pearls. 'They must be quite valuable. I suppose they're insured?'

'Is that all you can find to say about them?' Caroline heard herself snap, and was instantly contrite. Ashamed, too. 'I'm sorry, Jeremy darling. I'm a bit tired and fractious tonight, I'm afraid. Don't take any notice of my moods.'

'Of course you're tired, sweetie. My fault really, for coming along with the champagne. You must be whacked. Yesterday was a very long day, and you were under stress, too. No one can take a selection board in their stride, exactly. Or no one I've ever met. And you haven't eaten tonight, either. You must be starving.'

He was so nice. So understanding. She was so lucky.

Ginny came swishing downstairs in purple and gold – an embroidered caftan from Morocco – and they went into the dining room to consume – off the small round table Ginny had imported and placed in the bay window with a view of the lawns and the distant hills – a delicious cold collation, ending with peaches in brandy. By then Caroline, full of good food washed down by Jeremy's champagne, was relaxed, content, seeing life through a rosy glow. Jeremy's eyes caressed her, and she was warmed by his love. She knew herself beautiful tonight – and he was the one who had brought this about. He had given her security and confidence, and with him this was how the future would be. She fingered her mother's pearls and smiled across the table, her own eyes soft.

Her father watched Ginny, dark and unusually seductive in her Moroccan embroidery. 'Thank you, my darling,' he said to her, 'for this splendid meal. I think we might skip coffee, don't you? It would only keep us awake.'

'Yes, and Caroline must be worn out,' Jeremy agreed at once. 'It does wonders for her looks, I know, but she ought to be asleep.'

Robert regarded his daughter affectionately. Tonight she could do no wrong. A year or two at the Central, and then she'd be settled in Stonebridge with Jeremy, raising his grandchildren. Ginny could divide the house into two – she'd enjoy doing that – and they could all live under one roof, yet in two households. He'd lost his dearest Peggy, but he'd refused to be defeated. He put up a stupendous effort, remade his life, and now he was being rewarded. An idea struck him. 'With Caroline in London, we'll have a flat at our disposal,' he informed Ginny. 'A London *pied-à-terre*. How'll you like that? We can spend nights in town occasionally, go to a show or two, eh? How about it?'

Ginny backed him up excitedly – less, to be truthful, on account of the theatre trips than because of the light in his eyes as he planned this new interest. She'd worked with him for years, had loved him and understood him, and she had no illusions about the struggle he'd put up to re-establish himself with her.

'Take a nice big flat, Caroline,' he said expansively. 'I'll subsidize the rent. Find somewhere comfortable, so that we can come and spend weekends there. Dare say Jeremy won't mind coming with us, either.' He positively twinkled – something she'd not seen him do for years – at his future son-in-law. It was the twinkle that kept Caroline silent. She'd opened her mouth to say she'd already found a flat, that she'd pay for it herself, but that she'd be pleased to book them into a nearby hotel whenever they wanted to come for the weekend. But she bit back the words. Her father was as thrilled as a child over his new venture, and, like Ginny, she wanted to encourage him.

Jeremy was keen as mustard, too. 'What a super idea,' he said. 'I think that would be great. London weekends for us all.'

8

Caroline and Sarah

The next morning, Ginny apologized to Caroline. 'I'm dreadfully sorry about this London flat idea that got so much out of hand last night. It must seem a fearful bore – I'm sure you'd rather have your flat to yourself. But if you could bear with Robbie, I do think it would make such a difference to him.'

Caroline, too, had been pondering the situation, and reluctantly come to the same conclusion. 'I don't mind,' she said.

'I don't think you quite realize how important you are to him. You're part of his old life. Before me, I mean.' Ginny was always honest. 'He's settled with me now, but at the same time he still misses your mother, you know.'

Caroline didn't know what to say.

'You needn't pretend.' Ginny was unusually sharp. 'Of *course* he misses your mother. More than thirty years, they had. I'm an extra, not a substitute. Now he's going to miss you as well. He'd set his heart, you see, on having you here with him, as well as me.'

'But surely *you* can see I can't hang around for ever, simply to prop him up?'

'I can see all right. But Robbie can't. For one thing, he's jealous – I know it seems ridiculous, but it's true – he's jealous of the Central. It's the hospital that takes you away from him. He's hopelessly inconsistent, of course, because he's terribly proud of your career, too. But if you could see your way to letting him have his head about the flat, it would make such a difference to him.'

'All right.'

'And you will let him contribute to the cost, won't you? He does so want to feel he's still partly responsible for you, idiotic as it must seem to you.'

'I suppose so.' Caroline couldn't pretend to be pleased.

'Sorry,' Ginny said. 'I know how you must feel.'

'I dare say I can lump a great chunk of financial assistance without having my life totally wrecked,' Caroline admitted, with a grin.

'Angel. It'll mean a lot to Robbie, you know. You're much loved and cherished – you may not realize how much.'

Too much, Caroline surprised herself by thinking. And now plainly there was going to be no question of taking over Daniel's small one-room flat. The sooner she told him so, the better. He'd have to find another tenant. Nervously, in the lunch hour, she rang him.

'Too small?' he snapped down the telephone. 'Your father wants somewhere he can stay at weekends? Theatres and concerts? *Opera?* I see.' Somehow he made it sound as though they were a family of oil-rich Arabs proposing to rent a suite in the Ritz and half a dozen boxes at Covent Garden. 'I knew it was bound to be too small for you,' he informed her dogmatically.

'It wouldn't have been. I would have liked to have taken it on for myself. If it hadn't been for my father – '

'No explanations required.' Daniel was damned if he was going to listen to another word about that impossible father of Caroline's. 'You've made yourself clear. You don't want the flat.'

'It was so kind of you to suggest – '

'Didn't. Nothing to do with me. Andrew's notion, if you remember.'

Caroline had had enough. 'Then I expect,' she told him, her voice as brusque as his own, 'you'll be relieved to have it back in your own hands, to dispose of as you will.' She had an unexpectedly vivid picture of his hands, and pushed it angrily away. She was well out of that, she told herself, putting the receiver down smartly in its cradle, and pulling a face at it. He was intolerable. She picked up the telephone again and rang the estate agent near the Central and asked to be put on their mailing list, naming an inordinately high top level of rent. If Daniel thought the rich Milnes were flinging their money about, living in opulent luxury, she'd show him. She'd get herself a flat that would throw him right off centre. To hell with him.

Her self-satisfaction would have evaporated if she'd known that at the Central Wily Walter was campaigning on her behalf, having extracted from his departing senior registrar the information that Caroline was not taking over his own flat, and the reason for this.

'Harcourt's having it ? What's he want it for ?'

Andrew refrained from replying, baldly, 'To live in,' substituting instead 'He does find his own flat on the small side, I believe.'

'Too small for him, too small for Caroline Milne. Or so I would have imagined.' Walter was peevish. He hated having his plans altered.

'She doesn't have to have it.'

'Got to live somewhere, hasn't she ?'

This being undeniable, Andrew gave brief thanks to heaven that in a month from now he'd be shot of Walter Berkeley for ever, and said, 'I dare say she'll find somewhere easily enough, sir, if Harcourt's flat doesn't suit her. But – '

'Do you ? I don't. And I see no grounds for your opinion. I recollect distinctly, in any case, asking you to let her have your flat, and I must say I'm a little surprised to find that you and Harcourt apparently saw fit to ignore the arrangement I'd taken the trouble to make.'

Oh Lord. Andrew saw how it was going to be, back-pedalled smartly, and went off to ring Daniel. 'Wily Walter,' he told him, 'is peeved with you and me. It's Harcourt and Marshall today. I don't mind too much, because, after all, I only have to stick it out for another few weeks, but I thought I ought to warn you.'

Daniel groaned. 'What have we done now?'

'It's my flat he's on about. He wanted it for Caroline. You remember, at the time he did say —'

'Tell him the bloody girl can have it,' Daniel snapped.

'Oh, I don't know that we have to go as far as that to humour him. But —'

'I've just had her on the line. My flat is too small for her anyway, she said. So —'

'Hell. Just what Wily Walter said.'

'Put-up job, no doubt.'

'You think she got on to him, and complained?'

'Stands out a mile. I know he's psychic sometimes, but today I reckon there's a completely rational explanation. You'd better let her have your flat — I'll hang on here for a bit. After all, I'm not going to sit around in the department for ever, am I? Playing second fiddle to Madam. No way. I'll need to be looking round in any case, so probably there wouldn't be much point in moving just now. No, you let Caroline have it.'

'Well, if you're sure . . .'

'Never more so. Consider it settled.'

Andrew Marshall trod swiftly back to Walter Berkeley's room and informed him that Daniel was prepared to re-linquish the flat to Caroline.

'Good. Good. Right thing to do. Glad he's seen reason. Though I can't understand why you both had to — well, well, never mind. Never mind. All right, Andrew, thank you. Tell Daniel I'm obliged to him.'

Christian names again. Restored to favour. Hiding a grin, Andrew went back to his clinic, while Wily Walter got straight on to Caroline and told her he'd arranged for her to have Andrew's flat. 'It'll suit you very well. Said so all along.'

Caroline didn't know what to say. There was nothing she wanted less than to prevent Daniel taking over Andrew's flat, but how to explain this to the smugly elated Dr Berkeley? 'I don't want to be responsible for stopping Daniel Harcourt from carrying out the arrangements he's made,' she began unhappily.

'Nonsense. Must see you fixed up properly when you come back to us. What I've said from the beginning. Don't see why they had to quibble my arrangements in the first place.'

Caroline saw it all. Typical. This was how Walter had always been — interfering, detailed, and autocratic. She made a feeble attempt to avoid taking on Andrew's flat, but she was doomed to fail, and was unsurprised to hear herself weakly promising to ring him and discuss the take-over. Unhappily she did this, apologizing.

'No need to blame yourself,' Andrew said easily. 'All Wily Walter's doing. We're used to him and his little ways — you can't have forgotten, surely?'

Caroline, a little tartly, said that if she had she'd been forcibly reminded. At the same time, though . . .

'Not to worry. Daniel doesn't mind. As he didn't get the post, he'll very likely be moving on, so he's not keen on changing flats, after all.'

This information didn't exactly make Caroline feel better. She'd done this to Daniel. No one else. So much for her dreams. Reality, when it came along, showed both herself and him in a different light from the golden glow her imagination had painted over them.

Thank God for real life and Jeremy. With him solidly

behind her, she'd be able to face the warring temperaments of the director and the assistant director, the sniping
of Daniel in the background, and any other problems the
Central might throw at her. A happy personal life, her
mother had always said, enabled you to take professional
upsets in your stride.

Now, like her mother, she had to put complications
over a London flat out of her mind, and return to the
demands of the Stonebridge practice – in particular to
the Wakefield family, whose future continued to bother
her. After afternoon surgery in one of the outlying villages,
she decided to drive back to Stonebridge via the caravan
site at Edge Side. Teatime, so both Mrs Wakefield and
Sarah should be there, with any luck.

But Sarah was alone in the caravan. She came rushing
to the door and flung it open before Caroline had a chance
to knock. When she saw who it was, though, her face
fell.

'Oh, Dr Milne I – I thought – '

'May I come in, Sarah? Is your mother here?'

'No. She's out. I thought you were her, you see.'

'Sorry. I expect she'll be along soon.'

'Yes, I'm sure she will,' Sarah agreed politely, her small
face closed now.

Caroline looked round. The van was neat and tidy, a
charming and frilly miniature home, with its eighteen-
inch curtains in a dainty flower print matching the seat
cushions. Today, too, it held an extra air of festivity. The
pottery jug on the shelf contained freshly picked wild
flowers from the fields, the rosebud china was set out in
readiness on the blue formica table, there were pink paper
napkins, chocolate biscuits and an iced cake. Hardly the
perfect meal for a diabetic.

'Someone's birthday?' Caroline asked. 'Yours, Sarah?'

Sarah shook her head vehemently. 'Mummy's,' she explained, and bit her lip. 'She's a bit late, but I don't suppose she'll be long.

'I expect something held her up. She wouldn't want to be late for her birthday tea, I'm sure.'

'No, she wouldn't. And – and her present.' Sarah, her face alight with pride, gestured at the parcel by Mrs Wakefield's plate, wrapped in red tissue paper and surmounted by a carefully arranged bunch of white clover. 'See?' she said. 'I found her a four-leafed clover, too. To bring her luck all the year. I hope it's not going to be dead before she comes. I did have it in water, but – '

'I'm sure she'll be along in a minute.'

'Yes, of course she will be.' Sarah was fierce, and it became only too plain to Caroline that neither of them believed a word they were saying.

'Where did she go? How late is she?'

'She was having lunch with Mr Alsop. A birthday lunch.'

'Mr Alsop?'

'He's Mum's friend.'

'Oh, I see.' But did she? Was she leaping to an unjustified conclusion?

Sarah was fidgeting with the cutlery on the little pull-down table. 'I – I haven't actually had my tea yet. I didn't want to start without Mum. Not on her birthday. But – '

Caroline looked at her watch. 'Five-thirty. What time do you usually have tea?'

'Five o'clock is the latest, really.' Sarah sounded guilty.

'Then you certainly mustn't wait any longer.' She'd waited too long already. In another quarter of an hour or so she'd be hypoglycaemic. Just as Caroline had feared, Sarah needed watching. How often did this sort of thing happen?

'No. I won't wait any more. It's a pity, when it's her

birthday.' Sarah's mouth drooped, and she reached in a dismal way for bread and butter.

'What do you have to drink?' Caroline was matter-of-fact, but her heart bled for Sarah, whose feelings she recognized easily, for during her own childhood similar disappointments had been routine. A planned celebration, but no sign of her mother, out on a case. Did this happen often to Sarah, too? Was she for ever hanging about, waiting for her mother to arrive for meals? It might explain a great deal, especially if Mrs Wakefield had a new boyfriend.

'When Mum's here I have tea with her,' Sarah was answering Caroline's enquiry. 'But it doesn't seem worth making a pot just for me. I could have milk, only then there may not be enough left for my glass at bedtime and breakfast.'

'I haven't had tea yet. Do you suppose I could have a cup with you? While we wait for Mum?'

'Oh, would you, Dr Milne?' Sarah brightened at once. 'I'll put the kettle on. Would you like a chocolate biscuit?' She proffered the plate proudly.

'I'd love one. Though what you're doing with them I can't imagine. Not on your diet sheet, that's for sure.'

'Oh, they're not for me.' The child seemed surprised, and Caroline judged she was being truthful. 'I bought them as a surprise for Mum. She loves chocolate biscuits, but she doesn't often buy them, because of me. So I got these for her birthday treat.'

The kettle began to steam, and Sarah made tea, clearly with accustomed expertise. She glanced at the little clock on the shelf alongside the flowers. 'It has to stand for three minutes,' she explained. 'That's how Dad liked it.' She took another rosebud cup and saucer from a small overhead cupboard. 'This is the best china. Usually we just have our mugs and the melamine plates.'

Caroline was asking herself if Mrs Wakefield, after a liquid lunch, was somewhere in the town still, stoned out of her mind. Or, alternatively, celebrating the occasion in Mr Alsop's bed, her daughter forgotten. 'What do you usually do in the evening, when Mum's out?' she asked, drawing a bow at a venture.

Sarah was casual. 'Oh, I read. Or listen to the radio. Sometimes I write to Dad.'

Caroline was swept by a surge of overwhelming anger and yearning. Anger with Mrs Wakefield, and a yearning to be able to change Sarah's life. Poor lonely Sarah, coping on her own. This small plain ten-year-old at that moment held Caroline securely in the palm of her somewhat grubby and ink-stained hand. She wanted to make up to Sarah for all that was lacking in her life – for her parents' neglect and her loneliness, as well as for her medical problems. Alone in the caravan in the evening, writing faithfully to her father. Caroline could have wept. Instead she asked for bread and butter.

'Oh, *Doctor*.' Sarah was disappointed. 'Won't you have a chocolate biscuit instead? There are plenty, I bought a whole box.'

'Later, if I may. But I'm jolly hungry, so I think I'd like some bread and butter first.'

Sarah handed the plate across.

Caroline helped herself, and spread peanut butter, wondering what she was going to do when surgery hour arrived. Leave Sarah on her own? Obviously it wouldn't be the first time, or the last. But it seemed amazingly heartless simply to accept her tea, and then drive off. However, in the meantime, she could at least do a little investigating.

'Do you write to Dad often?'

Sarah nodded.

'Do you miss him?'

Sarah nodded again, and her eyes filled with an almost

adult pain, so that once more Caroline experienced that surge of poignant yearning. Sarah at ten reminded her so much of herself, she could so easily identify both with her loneliness and her independence. In the long term there might be no answers, but here and now she could surely offer comfort? 'How about coming round here and sitting next to me on this couch, and telling me more about Dad?'

Wordlessly, Sarah came round the table and sat down, stiff and bristly, but very close to Caroline. 'He lives with his new wife. Sue. Mum doesn't like her.'

'No, I dare say not.'

'But I do. I think she's super. I'd like to live with Dad and Sue, but Dad said Mum needed me here. Because she's not good on her own.'

'Oh, isn't she?'

'No, she needs me to look after her. Dad's quite right. For instance, she'd never get up in the morning, or make herself breakfast, if I wasn't here.'

'Wouldn't she?'

'No. She gets depressed on her own. But if I'm here, I get up when the alarm goes, and she gets up too, to give me my injection, and then once she's up, she's all right, you see, for the rest of the day.'

'It does sound as if she needs you.'

'Oh yes, she does. Perhaps she'll marry Mr Alsop, though.'

'Do you think she might?'

'Well, they seem very *interested* in each other.' Sarah's peaky little face was humorously tolerant of the ways of young love. 'I don't know if it'll come to anything.'

'Would you like it to?'

'Not if it means living with Mr Alsop,' Sarah said promptly. 'I'd rather be here on my own with Mum. But if it meant I could go and live with Dad and Sue, I'd like that.' She eyed Caroline briefly, and remarked casually 'it's a bit lonely here, you see.'

'I can imagine.' Caroline put an arm round Sarah, not at all sure she wouldn't be rebuffed, and hugged her.

Sarah didn't pull away, as Caroline had half-expected. Instead the flood-gates opened. 'I went to see Dad and Sue,' she said on a sudden burst of confidence, and clutched Caroline as if she were drowning. 'But they weren't there. They'd gone away.' Her eyes implored Caroline for reassurance. 'I didn't tell Mum. It would have upset her. You're the only person who knows – you won't say, will you?'

'Not if you don't want me to. When was this?'

'The day I should have gone to the hospital.'

'But – but I thought you overslept? And didn't go to London? Did you go to see Dad instead?'

'Not exactly. I didn't oversleep, 'smatter of fact. I never do. Mum only said that because she thought it sounded better.'

'Better than what?'

'You won't say? You won't tell?'

Oh dear. Suppose she had to? 'Not if I can help it,' Caroline promised cautiously.

'It's a bit complicated. First of all, you see, Mum wasn't here anyway. She'd gone to stay with Mr Alsop.'

'Oh, had she?' Caroline said grimly.

'Yes. She said she'd be back in time to take me to the hospital. Mr Alsop would drive us to the station in his van, she said.'

'But he didn't?'

'They were late. I don't suppose Mr Alsop realized about Mum not waking up in the morning. So when it got near the time and they hadn't come, I thought I'd go on my own. I caught the bus to the station, and bought my ticket out of the house-keeping purse, and went on the train.'

Caroline was lost in admiration. 'That was perfectly splendid of you,' she said. 'I think you did magnificently.'

'Oh, do you?' Sarah flushed. 'I started off all right, I know, but then when I got to London, there were so many people and so much traffic, I wasn't sure I could find the way to the hospital on my own, so I decided to go and fetch Dad to go with me. I know exactly how to go from Waterloo to the flat, you see. I've done it again and again, when we used to spend weekends here.'

'I see. And then he wasn't there?'

Sarah nodded. It had been the worst blow of her short life. Worse even than her parents' separation. 'I arrived there, and somebody different opened the door.'

Haltingly, she told Caroline about it. Or about some of it. There were parts she left out. She didn't tell Caroline, for instance, how happy she'd been until that moment. Walking through the familiar streets again had been lovely, and she'd pretended to herself she was living in the flat with Dad and Sue. She'd walked confidently up the stairs to the familiar door and rung the bell, thinking of the fuss and excitement there'd be when they realized it was her. But then the door had been opened by a stranger. Sarah had stared, at a loss – at first she'd checked on the number, imagining she must have gone one floor too far by mistake. But she hadn't. This was the right flat. She'd asked for her father, carefully, by his name. 'Could I see Mr Wakefield, please?'

'Oh, they don't live here any more.'

'Not live here?'

'No, they've moved further out.'

'Oh.' Sarah hadn't known what to do. It had been the woman – kindly, and a little perturbed – who had offered the address. Sarah had thanked her and taken it.

'Will you be all right?'

'Oh yes, perfectly all right, thank you.' Sarah had wanted only to get away without a fuss. She was determined not to cry in front of the stranger. 'Stiff upper lip, sweetheart,' she could hear her father saying. Hemel Hempstead. He and Sue had gone to Hemel Hempstead. They'd left without telling her.

She was going to cry. She had to find somewhere away from people – she couldn't be walking around in tears. The park would do. Sniffing and blowing her nose, she walked along the well-known streets. This had been home, and she'd thought, until a few minutes ago, that it was still home. That she'd find Dad and Sue, and the familiar flat, even if she couldn't stay with them. Memories crowded of the old days, and her throat was tight with the urge to break down and cry. But it would never do to cry in the road in front of everyone. She had to hide. At last she reached the park, made her way to the shrubbery where she'd played so often when she was younger, almost a kindergarten baby, and crept through to the inner sanctum among the dry branches of the laurel, where finally she let it all come rushing out, the pain and misery and disappointment.

When she had cried herself out, a sort of tranquillity took over. She sat up, and for comfort, as well as to brace herself for the loneliness ahead, she began pretending – an only child, she was adept at filling the hours with long day-dreams. She'd gone to the flat, and it had all been quite different. Dad and Sue were there. Dad took her to the hospital for her appointment, and then she went back to the flat with him, and they all had a scrumptious meal, cooked by Sue – the hospital had told her she was better, and from now on she could eat *anything*, and never have another injection. After the meal, Dad told her she was going to stay with them, because Mum would be all right now with Mr Alsop.

It was a lovely long pretend, and it set her up. But then she had to face it. It was only pretend. Dad and Sue had gone to this place, Hemel Hempstead. She didn't know how to get there, or if she had enough money for the fare. Where was it? Further out, the lady had said. What she ought to do was to go to the hospital. That was what she had come to London for. But she didn't know how to find it from here – she'd relied on Dad to see to that.

She'd have to go home to Stonebridge. And she'd better hurry up about it, too. She had brought some sugar with her, and it was time she ate it. Grubby and streaked with tears, she sat in the shrubbery munching sugar and planning her return methodically. When she arrived at Waterloo she could go to the kiosk and buy biscuits. That way she ought to last out until she reached home. She'd tell Mum she'd tried to go to the hospital and lost herself. Better not say anything about having tried to join Dad and Sue. It would only upset her.

An expurgated version of this saga – leaving out the shrubbery bit, and the tears – was related to Caroline, who listened attentively, asked questions now and again, and finally said, 'It must have been awful for you, Sarah. I am so sorry.'

'You aren't annoyed?'

'What about?'

'Mum said you would be. Because I didn't keep my appointment. That's why she said we'd better tell you we'd never set off. Because it was a bit feeble of me, I know, to get to London all right and then not to go to the hospital. I told Mum I lost my way – I didn't say anything about going to find Dad, because she would only have been cross. She didn't like Dad and Sue living in our flat.'

'No, I can imagine she might not.'

'Even though she knows it's her own fault.'

'Her own fault?'

'For leaving him alone so much. That's what she says herself. To come down here, she thinks, because she liked it better here always. But I think it was more because Mum never used to get proper meals. Sue worked with Dad, and she started to come and cook for all of us – Mum's no good at cooking, of course. She doesn't like it, and then she forgets about it, too. But Sue's a jolly good cook. She's pretty super all round, in fact. Poor Mum hadn't a chance, especially as Dad had been fed up with her for a long time – she was always complaining and wanting to move.'

With very little encouragement, Sarah poured it all out. How Mum had never been able to get up in the morning, and Sarah and her Dad used to get breakfast together. He'd give her her injection, too, and take her to school on his way to work. And Mum was for ever moaning about how she couldn't stand London, the noise and dirt, and why couldn't Dad look for a job in the country, and they could have a nice house and a garden. 'But he said he'd got a good job, and he wasn't going to lose it, so he bought the caravan for weekends and holidays. And Mum liked it down here, and in the end we used to stay here all the time for the school holidays. Dad came down on Friday night and went back early on Monday morning. Mum said it was good for me to be out of London, and she was doing it for my sake, but she wasn't, it was for herself. And it wasn't even particularly good for me, because she kept forgetting to do the shopping, and I had to keep on reminding her about my injections and my diet. It was much better in the flat with Dad to see to everything.'

Caroline sighed. 'Yes, I dare say it was.'

'Of course, I was much younger then. It was a long time ago, you see. Anyway, in the end Dad said I'd better go to school down here, and then after a bit he stopped coming down every weekend. And then one day when he did come he said he and Mum were going to have a divorce, but it wouldn't make any difference to me, because I'd still have both of them, and I could go and see him at the weekend, instead of him coming to see me. So I did, and it was super, and I kept asking him if I couldn't live in the flat again with him and Sue. But he said not, because Mum would be so upset. He said he'd let her down in a way, and he was sorry about it, but I mustn't go off too.' Sarah scowled. 'Only I think it was Mum who let him down. But I knew Dad was right, and I'd have to stay with her. So I said I would. But I do wish I didn't have to.'

Caroline echoed her wish.

The following morning, after surgery, she gave Alan Peterson a résumé of her conversation with Sarah. 'Obviously,' she ended disgustedly, 'Mrs Wakefield used to neglect Sarah and her husband, and now she's still neglecting Sarah – probably thinking all the time about having it off with Mr Bloody Alsop. And as I shall have left by then, you're going to be the one who'll have to see that somehow or other Sarah gets to her next appointment at the Central. I suggest you get out to the caravan in time to prepare breakfast for them, and then drive them to the station.'

'Well,' Alan said seriously, 'I might at that. Drive them to the station, anyway. With any luck, if I tell her I'll do that, they'll both be there ready and waiting.'

9

Senior Registrar at the Central

When Caroline began work at the Central she was already the focus of intense speculation. She was, one story went, Walter Berkeley's girlfriend, brought back to the department over the head of the leading candidate for her post, Daniel Harcourt. On the contrary, others maintained, she was Daniel's ex-girlfriend, who had snatched the post from under his nose at the eleventh hour, so that now he no longer wanted to know her. Here both stories came together. She had dropped Daniel, they said, because, with an eye to the future, she was now busily engaged in pursuing Wily Walter, who had in any case always fancied her. With him behind her, what's more, she had snatched not only Daniel's post but the flat Andrew Marshall had promised him, too. It was all a shocking example of what happened when you let all these women into medicine, the men added, though with a glint in their eyes, and it must be admitted that both Daniel and Walter Berkeley had something. She was an extraordinarily good-looking girl, and it was not hard to understand why Wily Walter was for once as putty in those long-fingered capable hands.

And what, they began asking one another as soon as she appeared in the department for her first day's work, was that socking great rock on her finger? Had someone beaten Wily Walter to the post? Surely he, who grudged paying out so much as a cup of coffee if he could avoid it, would never have come across with that? And Daniel could never have afforded it – he hadn't a bean apart from his salary.

'Some unknown character called Jeremy,' Dr Berkeley's house physician was able to inform them by lunchtime.

Daniel was annoyed to find himself amazingly put out by the news, which reached him with the speed of light, though he wasn't in the residents' common room at lunch and hadn't so far set eyes on Caroline herself.

So what had he expected? Because he'd had this weird feeling for her ever since he'd set eyes on her, was she supposed to hold herself inviolate? He should be so lucky. In any case, the dreams he'd cherished of her were insane. They'd been idiotic two years ago, when he'd gone down to Stonebridge only to be more or less shown the door by that devilish father of hers, and they were even dottier now, when she'd not only taken the post he'd wanted, but had refused, with her nose in the air, the offer of his flat. Too small for her.

Well, it was too small, that was why he'd been moving out. As well as for other reasons, now best forgotten. For on top of everything she was flaunting about the hospital flashing this great enormous diamond about like a neon sign.

She certainly needn't suppose she'd ever have got anything like that from him. Vulgar. Ostentatious. Jeremy someone, she'd got herself engaged to. What a rotten sort of name that was. Affected. Pretentious.

They met on the ward round in the afternoon, greeted one another with frigid formality. Daniel in fact was still digesting the somewhat unpalatable results of a conversation he'd had with Sir Graham on his way up to the ward.

'Decided how you intend to proceed, eh?' Sir Graham had demanded in his thin pernickety voice.

'Proceed?' For a moment Daniel assumed him to be

asking which route they were to follow from the main hall to the ward.

'Since you didn't get the senior post.'

'Oh. Oh, that.'

'Yes. That. Or had it escaped y'r attention?'

'No. No, of course not, sir. It's just that – well, I don't know quite what to do, to be honest. It's not, of course, that I was actually counting on being appointed, or anything of that sort.' Not much it wasn't. But he'd die sooner than admit it, and fortunately he'd been careful to be scrupulously correct in any conversation about the appointment. It had been his friends who had, outwardly, taken it for granted the post was his. Never himself. So at least none of them could say – hell, he knew they were all saying it. But he'd never been a party to it, and he wasn't going to begin now. 'It's simply that while it was on the cards that I might be staying in the department, I didn't actually look for any posts away from here. I suppose I'll have to start looking. Pretty soon. Do you by any chance know of any post coming up, sir?' Perhaps that was what the old devil had been driving at.

'Not precisely, no. But in a year the post at Mortimer's will be vacant. I see no reason why you shouldn't put in for it, with my backing. And I could have a word, y'know.'

That meant that this time he probably could count on it. But a year ahead? What was he supposed to do in the meantime? Starve? A good thing, perhaps, that Caroline had taken over Andrew's flat. If he was supposed to live on air, while he hung around waiting for the Mortimer's post – which, of course, would be well worth waiting for – this was not the moment to start trying to run a large and comparatively expensive flat. 'Very good of you, sir. I'd appreciate that very much. I don't quite know what I'd do between now and then, though.'

'Well, now, I was rather wondering if you wouldn't stay

on here with me for a further year, y'know. It would suit me very well, and I dare say we could arrange it without any difficulty. I see no reason why we shouldn't.'

'I see. Thank you very much, sir.' He'd better grab the offer while the old boy was in the mood. 'I'd be most grateful. I'd like to do that.' He wouldn't. He'd hate it. But clearly the Mortimer's post was going to depend on his remaining with Sir Graham for the intervening period. And, after all, why not? It had suited him up to now, and surely he wasn't so reactionary that he was unable to endure a woman in a senior post over him? Or was it Caroline herself he couldn't endure?

He must put this nonsense behind him, become strictly impersonal. Professional.

He hadn't, however, succeeded in putting it behind him when he and Sir Graham arrived at the ward, and he gave Caroline an extremely bleak look.

Quaking with nerves in any case, she offered an icy smile in response, her condition in no way improved by Daniel's quelling glare. She set her lips, and sailed forward, apparently with total self-possession, to greet the professor.

Since she had prepared herself with enormous thoroughness, the round went like a dream, and even Sister was faintly impressed. So, to his intense irritation, was Daniel. Of course, she'd always been good, his Caro, but – his Caro? He surely to God couldn't still be mad enough to be thinking of her along these lines?

He could. He was. However, he was going to cease doing so forthwith. If not sooner. She was an extremely able colleague, who in due course was going to marry someone called Jeremy – God knew why. What a waste. She'd no doubt retire from medicine, the silly girl, and start producing kids. However, none of it, luckily, had anything to do with him. Her affairs had ceased to be any concern of his nearly two years ago, after she'd gone into that practice of her mother's. Evidently that had failed to work out, as he could have told her at the time. In fact, he had told her. He'd gone down there all set to drag her back to the Central by her hair, too, only to be greeted by what amounted to a family conspiracy to freeze him out. The memory made him shudder. He'd handled the situation hopelessly, of course. He could see that now. But he'd returned to London at the end of what seemed then – and now – like the worst weekend of his life with his emotions in tatters. Muddled, angry and – he flinched from the word, but no other filled the bill – heartbroken. And after that he'd had measles. As soon as he recovered, he'd devoted a good deal of time and energy to restoring his sagging morale and filling the hideous gap Caroline had left – mainly with work, with one or two tentative forays towards opening an affair. But a bare six weeks before she'd turned up at that damned interview, he'd been forced to admit the truth. Only Caroline would do. The gap in his life was caused by her absence.

He'd decided to make another approach. But, idiot that he'd been, he'd postponed getting in touch with her, because he'd stupidly imagined he was fairly sure of that blasted job and he'd seen himself, Lord High Everything, descending on Caro and her pompous silly old bastard of a father with his new post in his pocket. His new flat, too, ready for her. The need for the flat, of course, it came to him suddenly, had been the direct result of the blow to his self-confidence administered by that one solitary visit to Burvale. He'd felt he had to have a suitable home ready and waiting, as well as a position in life to offer her. He'd imagined himself, the departmental senior registrar from the teaching hospital, penetrating into rural fastnesses to collect his forsaken girlfriend, languishing in the provinces as an assistant in some run-down general practice.

He'd fallen flat on his face and it served him right. For it was Caro, his darling brilliant Caro in person, who had rescued herself without any assistance from anyone, sweeping back into the Central and his life and snatching both job and flat from under his astonished nose.

So now here they both were. And it was beginning to dawn on him that this was all that mattered. To hell with senior posts and who owned which flat. He and Caro were once again walking the wards of the Central together. So she'd dealt his prestige a blow. Good for her. He didn't care. He could pick himself up and fight another day.

That was his Caro. She'd show them all. He was proud of her. On the ward round he'd even been a little edgy, wondering if she was going to be up to this post she'd landed, or if he ought to have taken her on one side beforehand, given her a bit of quiet coaching, filled in the background for her, warned her about one or two pitfalls.

But she could look after herself. She was doing all right. What he had to do was get in there fighting, grab the blasted girl back before that damned Jeremy in Stonebridge whose vulgar great ring she was wearing finally got around to making an honest woman of her.

This thought, instead of depressing him, put him into tearing high spirits. The campaign stretched invitingly ahead, daily life had brilliance and sparkle. He was going places, Caro with him, and be blowed to anyone who got in his way. Jeremy Whosit, here I come.

And at that very moment round the corner came Caroline. He promptly astounded her by offering, instead of the bleak look he'd thrown cuttingly in her direction before the ward round, a warm smile. 'Hey,' he said. 'I was thinking about you. Where are you off to? Got a moment to spare?'

'Well, I – ' She was thrown. 'I suppose I – actually I'm not – '

'Great.' Even listening to her waffle was a delight. His Caro. In some sort of state of nerves – presumably the rigour of the ward round had caught up with her, and she was paying the price now it was all over. 'That's splendid.'

He was exuding reassurance from every pore – she might, she thought, have been a frightened child he was chatting up, from the amount of warmth and encouragement he was directing at her. It came across in waves, and she found herself drinking it up, insensibly relaxing, almost basking in the joy of being with him again. Her responsibilities, that had been weighing her down a moment earlier, fell away, and she felt renewed. What on earth was happening to her? And what was he up to?

He told her. 'We ought to have a party.'

'A – a party?' Who ought to, for God's sake? The department, or simply the two of them? Or had he already landed a senior post somewhere else? In Saudi Arabia, with a huge salary, perhaps, or the Mayo Clinic? That must be it. That would account for the unexpected change in attitude, too. He was off, leaving the Central for ever. None of them mattered any more. He was talking about his farewell party. Her spirits collapsed.

'To celebrate your return to the Central, and your new post,' he explained, watching her.

Caroline gagged. This was too much. 'Ug – ugh – wha – my p-p-post?' she stammered.

All at once he looked amazingly like Sir Graham Williamson at his most acerbic. 'Quite so. Though your response could be expressed with a little more clarity. Even coherence.'

'I'm sorry.' She had to laugh. They were in touch again, the uneasy formality of their recent encounters dissolved. They were back with the mutual understanding that had so much encouraged her when he'd first arrived at the Central. 'I thought you didn't like me getting it,' she was able to say honestly. 'So why should you want to celebrate?'

'I didn't like me not getting it,' he told her accurately enough. 'But you getting it is great. And needs celebrating, as I said. So when and where?'

'Well, I –'

'Tell you what, we'll have the party in my place, eh?'

'If you're sure –'

'Fix a date now, and I'll get some booze in. Bring that fiancé of yours along, of course.'

'Oh – er – yes.' Unaccountably, Caroline was put out. She found she didn't, to be truthful, want to bring Jeremy. She'd been assuming Daniel wanted her for herself alone, that he knew nothing about Jeremy – after all, she'd said nothing.

She must be a nut case. She was wearing Jeremy's ring, and there was always the grapevine. In any case, Daniel always knew all about everyone, often long before they knew it themselves. She remembered how they'd all been struck when, in his first days at the Central, he'd astonished them by his almost uncanny grasp of what everyone was up to – and why. 'Thank you,' she responded politely. 'I'll tell him.'

Daniel brandished his diary at her, gave her alternative dates, after which she obediently trotted off to telephone Jeremy, to find out which evening he could manage.

He was pleased at the prospect. 'Good,' he said. 'It'll be pleasant to go to a London party. I'll get away early, and we can have a meal first somewhere. How would that be?'

She was apologetic. 'You'd better not count on it, I'm afraid. I may not be able to get away in time.'

'I thought you said the party wouldn't start until nine?'
He was outraged.

'I know. But I may be held up in the wards. I think we'd better meet at the flat, if you don't mind. And then if I'm not there, you can help yourself to some supper.'

'Not much point,' he said disgustedly, 'in busting myself to leave early to have supper by myself in your flat. Might as well have a sandwich on the train. Will there be food at this party?'

'Daniel will be sure to have something laid on, even if it's only stacks of sandwiches from the canteen.'

Jeremy groaned, and pointed out somewhat acidly that none of this seemed worth a journey of two hundred miles.

Caroline couldn't help the spurt of relief, and told herself that this must be due to the fact that he'd almost certainly be the sole non-medical member of the group. A fish out of water. 'I'm afraid you'd probably find it fearfully boring, anyway,' she assured him. 'Nothing but talk about patients, drug dosages and path tests. It probably isn't worth the journey, as you say.'

Perversely, he at once insisted on attending the party, telling her firmly he'd see her at the flat about eight o'clock.

When he arrived, he presented her with an orchid.

Caroline, who'd reached the flat in a rush only ten minutes earlier, and had climbed into her patterned velvet, with a discreet shirt she considered suitable for the senior registrar, gaped uncertainly at the flower.

'Don't you like it?'

'Yes, Jeremy. Yes, darling, of course I do.' Only it's not quite Central style, or suitable for a cheerful departmental get-together in Daniel's flat. A bit embarrassing in fact. But how touching of Jeremy to have thought of it. Even if it was out of place, what the hell? She kissed him, praying that he wasn't going to be able to spot that

116

her unusual demonstrativeness came from guilt rather than joy. 'It's just that no one's ever thought of giving me an orchid before. Have you eaten?'

'On the train.'

'Oh, good. Perhaps we'd better be on our way – I'll have to rely on Daniel's sandwiches.

However, Daniel, during Caroline's absence, had advanced from canteen sandwiches to spaghetti bolognese in a great dish brought over from Giovanni's, the little Italian eating place much patronized by Central staff, followed by a well-filled cheese board and long French bread, from the same source.

'Super food, Daniel,' Caroline congratulated him, as she toyed, replete, with a small and delicious morsel of cheese covered with walnuts.

He refilled her glass from the heavy ship's decanter he'd also acquired since her day, and collapsed into a sprawl at her feet. 'Glad you liked it,' he said, and stretched his legs out with a sigh of relief. 'My feet are killing me, so I'll stay here with you now. I've done my duty, filled them up with food and drink to the eyebrows, so now I'm entitled to stay and chat up my favourite girl.' Cosily, he leant his head back against her patterned velvet.

His touch sent happiness surging through her, though her eyes, uneasily, travelled across the room, searching for Jeremy.

Daniel followed her gaze. 'Your beloved,' he said sarcastically, 'seems to be doing OK.'

Caroline saw that Jeremy was deeply engrossed in conversation with a luscious blonde. She fought a piercing desire to run her fingers through Daniel's hair and cradle his head in her arms. She fought a rising sense of panic, too, and almost wished Jeremy would drop the blonde and come charging across the room to rescue her. 'It's only,' she explained weakly – and inaccurately – 'that he doesn't know anyone, and I – '

'Does now.' Daniel was off-hand.

'Yes, of course. But he's the only non-medical – '

'Don't require to be medical to chat up dizzy blondes.'

'No. No, I suppose not.'

Daniel, she remembered, had always possessed this knack of carrying on, in a quiet but audible undertone, a detailed conversation against a background of unearthly din. Round them the department screeched like the parrot house at the zoo, but Daniel, having disposed of Jeremy, proceeded to unload the case history of a thirteen-year-old with fibrocystic disease. From this it was a short step to relate, in her turn, her own problems over Sarah Wakefield – who was booked to come up to Walter Berkeley's outpatients the following week. 'I'd really like to admit her for observation, if we could,' she explained. 'But it would be mainly on social grounds, I'm afraid.' She pulled a face. 'I don't know how Walter would take that.'

Daniel snorted. 'You've no problem there. Just open your eyes wide – that's right, like now – and talk. Twist him round your little finger whenever you choose.'

'He's certainly being amazingly amenable so far. I'm waiting for it to wear off.'

'Your fatal fascination overpowers him.' Daniel heard himself being sarcastic again, and asked himself why he had to sound as though he despised Caroline's appeal, when in fact it was even more effective when used on him than on Walter Berkeley. Why couldn't he tell her so, instead of churning out snide remarks? But somehow he couldn't bridge the gap, and was only able to prevent himself from sniping at her by diverging into departmental gossip. 'Anyway,' he added truthfully, 'he's probably so relieved to have you around instead of Andrew that everything is sunny-side-up at present. He and Andrew had been getting across one another recently, you know. Andrew has been a bit big for his boots recently – thought he knew it all. In a way he did, too. But a mistake to make it so clear.'

'Andrew was amazingly good – I'm petrified when I remember it's his job I've got. Sometimes I wake up at night, and I can hardly believe it. All the same, I can hardly believe, either, that I've been away for two years. Now I'm back it feels as if I've been here for ever. And yet – '

'Except for old Jerrikins over there, presumably.'

'He's not called Jerrikins.' Caroline was cross. She looked indignantly across the room, and was unreasonably put out to see Jeremy in the act of clinking glasses with the blonde.

'Dietician,' Daniel said briefly.

'Er – what?'

'The blonde. You used not to be so slow. Perhaps Jerrikins no sort of stimulus towards cerebration? Fenella Jamieson.'

'I see.' Caroline tried to be cold and disapproving, but caught his eye and grinned halfway.

'Anytime.' Daniel was airy. He removed his head from her skirt, turned on his side, and lounging on one arm reached for a saucer of twiglets and offered them to her with a lift of his dark brows.

Dreamily, Caroline took one.

Daniel crunched up a good handful, and Caroline recollected that he had an inordinate passion for them.

He was watching her quizzically. 'That an orchid you're wearing?' he demanded.

'Yes.' Caroline flushed.

'Jerrikins?'

'I do wish you wouldn't – oh, all right. Yes.'

Daniel lapsed into silence, which Caroline took to be condemnation of her ostentatious dressing. She never guessed that the flower had depressed him, had brought home to him inescapably his own inadequacy and lack of sophistication. He would never, in ten years, he knew, have thought of buying Caroline an orchid.

To her, though, he seemed to be brimming with all the vitality and confidence she remembered, and she had not a suspicion even that he was growing, as the evening advanced, steadily more miserable and pessimistic – as well as bitterly jealous. He was certain of only one depressing fact. He'd had his chance and lost it. Two years ago, he'd let her slip through his fingers. Because he'd allowed himself to be frightened off by her pompous old father and that great mausoleum of a house. But how could he now suppose he was going to detach her from that smooth and affluent bloke on the other side of the room? Until he'd met Jeremy, to recapture Caroline had seemed the work of a moment. A moment or two together, and they'd be back where they started. But now Jeremy had reality and substance. and Daniel had no more faith in himself. In due course Jeremy would detach himself from his passing encounter with Fenella, he'd claim Caroline, and they'd go off together into the night, an established couple.

As it happened, their departure turned out to be a good deal less upsetting than Daniel had expected, as Jeremy suddenly discovered he was going to miss the last train to Stonebridge unless he grabbed a taxi almost instantly. Caroline galloped out with him, sure enough, but it was plain that she was going to wave goodbye within seconds.

In fact, they picked up a taxi easily near the hospital entrance, and it bore Jeremy swiftly away to Waterloo.

Caroline walked slowly back along the square to her own flat. Well fed and well wined, she should, she told herself, be relaxed and content. She had just had her celebration party with the department, she had the job she wanted, and she was engaged to Jeremy. Kind, reliable Jeremy. What more could anyone want?

Daniel.

No doubt of it, he still possessed that uncomfortable power over her. As he'd stretched out beside her tonight, not even bothering to be particularly agreeable and picking on Jeremy – Jerrikins, indeed – and arguing with her about what to do next with the fibrocystic child, she'd been aware of him as she was never aware of Jeremy.

He wasn't even especially good-looking.

Jeremy was better-looking, she thought firmly.

Daniel was –

She had to stop thinking about Daniel. She was engaged to Jeremy, who would be a good person to go through life with, to share the upbringing of children. She liked him and admired him, and she'd promised to marry him. And meant it, too.

So she had to get over Daniel. She had to turn her back on this tumult in body and mind, this restless hunger to hold him to her for ever. Surely she could think of him as a valued friend, as a pleasant and intelligent colleague. Like, say, Alan Peterson.

Like Alan Peterson?

There could be no one less like Alan. Daniel was a disturbance. His dark eyes mocked her now, sat enshrined somewhere in her head, staring right into her soul, undermining her resolution.

Daniel and Jeremy

Daniel had been right about Sarah Wakefield. A day or two later, in outpatients, Walter agreed to admit her for observation. 'If you think it's necessary,' he said to Caroline, who'd just completed an account of Sarah's past history and her caravan home. He turned to the assembled students. 'You heard Dr Milne's opinion. You noted her knowledge of the background. Too many of you forget that patients have homes, or any life at all for that matter, away from here. The child lives in a caravan, goes into hypoglycaemic coma. We must have her in for investigation.' Daniel winked at Caroline.

A week later, Sarah was admitted. Mrs Wakefield brought her up, and was still sitting with her in the ward when Daniel and Johnny Waller, on the way out after seeing one of Sir Graham's new admissions, stopped by her bed. 'I think this must be the case Dr Milne was telling me about,' Daniel said. 'Hang on a minute, Johnny.'

Obediently his houseman pulled up short, glanced at his watch. This was supposed to be his free evening, and they'd another ward to get through.

'Hullo, Mrs Wakefield and Sarah, is it?'

'Yes, Doctor, that's right.'

'I'm Dr Harcourt. I – '

'I was going to see Dr Milne,' Sarah interrupted, rude because she'd gone into instant panic. 'You said Dr Milne would be here to look after me.' She glared accusingly at her mother.

'I'm sure she'll be along, Sarah. Be a bit patient,' Mrs Wakefield told her. 'She's known Dr Milne quite a while, you see,' she added apologetically, worried that Sarah had already antagonized this forceful young man.

'It was Dr Milne who told me about you, Sarah,' Daniel was comforting. 'She'll be along to see you herself as soon as she can, so not to worry. In fact, I see her now. 'Look.' He pointed down the ward.

Caroline's tall figure, white-coated, came fast through the swing doors, homed on to Sarah's bed. 'Hullo, Sarah,' she said briskly. 'And Mrs Wakefield. You got here all right. That's good.'

'Dr Peterson took us to the station in his car,' Sarah said importantly. Caroline's mouth twitched – Alan had taken her instructions seriously, something she'd not expected. 'And then we went in the train and the tube.' Sarah, immensely cheered to see her, was bouncing up and down in bed. 'And I've got smashing new pyjamas – see?'

'That's enough, Sarah. Calm down, do.' Mrs Wakefield was fussed. The new white-coated Dr Milne in her hospital intimidated her in a manner Dr Milne from the Hollies had never done. 'Don't bother the doctor with all that.'

'That's a super anorak, too. Is that new as well?'

'Well, not for here especially. But I –'

'She *would* wear it.' Mrs Wakefield was even more fussed. 'I wanted her to bring a proper dressing gown, but –'

'I couldn't wear that old thing.' Sarah was scornful. 'This is much better.' She'd had one of her rare rows with her mother over the dressing-gown problem. Mrs Wakefield had bought her new pyjamas for the hospital, and a sponge bag, as well as a suitcase – the two of them had spent a splendid afternoon in Broomhurst picking out all this gear – but there had not been enough in the kitty for a new dressing gown, too. 'Your old one is far too shabby,' Mrs Wakefield had worried. 'All stained, and it won't wash out. Too short, too. Tell you what, you can have mine.' This was a sacrifice, but it went unappreciated.

'I can't wear that,' Sarah was dogmatic.

'I'll shorten it, you'll see, and it'll be all right. You'll look very nice in it.'

'No. I'm not going to have it.'

'Why not? What's wrong with it?' Mrs Wakefield was offended. She was very fond of her housecoat, and the offer to make it over for Sarah had not come easily to her.

'Oh, it's all right for you, I suppose.' Sarah's voice was that of superior daughters everywhere with frumpy old mums in dowdy outfits. Mrs Wakefield, only twenty-eight and going great guns with Mr Alsop, was shaken. 'But I'd look stupid in it. It's got that awful lace on, and those itsy-bitsy rosebuds. Ugh.'

'You might at least say thank you. It's not my idea of fun, losing my housecoat for you and that wretched hospital.'

'Don't, then. I don't want it. Me, in that. I'd be a giggle.' Nothing was going to induce Sarah to cross the threshold of the Central London Hospital, far less meet her Dr Milne, in such a sissy garment. 'I can wear my anorak, same as I do here most of the time.'

'I can't imagine what Dr Milne is going to think. You ought to have a proper dressing gown.'

'Well, I haven't got one, have I? So there.'

Full circle. The conversation was repeated, more acrimoniously the second time round. Finally, though, Sarah had her way, and now sat triumphantly in bed, preening herself in her anorak before Dr Milne and three other doctors, all of whom dutifully made admiring noises before going off down the ward together.

'How about a meal when we're through here, Caro-'

Daniel asked, as they were passing through to the opposite ward.

'Well, Ginny and my father are supposed to be coming up for a theatre. They – '

'For God's sake, woman,' Daniel pointed, 'you see that black thing there on the wall? It's known as a telephone. You pick it up, and – '

Caroline laughed, and finally agreed that she'd ring Ginny and explain she'd probably be out when they arrived, but that she'd be in when they came back from the theatre.

Daniel took her to the Country Garden. Belatedly, as part of his campaign to win Caroline back, he'd genned himself up on restaurants, consulting the senior registrar in neurology, known to be a reliable bloke who dined out well but not too spectacularly. 'Trouble is, I'm not any good at that sort of thing, Paul,' he'd confided – not that he'd needed to. The Central already knew it. 'So it's no use prescribing some jazzy place where they give the lady a flower and you have six waiters breathing down your neck. I'd only go to pieces. I pretty well go to pieces anyway, when I have to cope with a bird and a menu at the same moment. I lose my head.'

'Never seen you do that,' Paul Goddard had said.

'Never seen me in a restaurant, have you? I'm a dumb oaf.'

'Why on earth can't you feed the girl in your flat, then? I thought you were the clever laddie who had Giovanni's all lined up to zoom across the square with the good Italian home-cooking.'

'No.' Daniel was determined. 'I've got to begin sometime, and I'm beginning now, with Caro. If I can't do it for her, I'll never be able to.'

'Bad as that, is it?'

Daniel groaned. 'Worse. I could kick myself all round

the Central. Two years I've wasted, and she's acquired this damned accountant. I've got to get her away from him.'

'Right. Let's see. There's – no, perhaps that's a bit too gaudy. Tell you what, how about the Country Garden? That should do you nicely. Did a lot of my own courting there. Friendly place, with good food. That's it.'

So he took her there that evening, although he had a battle with himself before telephoning to book a table, fighting an urgent impulse to ring Giovanni's instead.

On his way along the square to fetch Caroline, he read himself a stern lecture. Don't gabble on everlastingly about drugs and case histories, he warned himself. Look into her eyes and draw her out. He knew how to draw a child out, after all. He could hold a child's hand and give it confidence and security. Any child in need in the wards or clinic could depend on him. He held nothing of himself back, and he had no problem in dispensing warmth, affection and love by the bucketful. But when it came to Caroline he clammed up and turned into a nervy egotist, wondering what she was thinking of him, whether she was bored, whether she'd far sooner be somewhere else with almost anyone else. Yet this was Caro. He knew her. He loved her. Two years ago – in another access of self-doubt – he threw away his chances with her. But luck had presented him with a second opportunity. He must take it. He must hold her hand, gaze into her eyes, those lovely deep eyes that he'd remembered through the missing years, and tell her he loved her and always would.

The Country Garden bit went all right. They were safely shown to a table, the prices were no shock because Paul had briefed him, and he persuaded Caroline to choose what they should eat. When it came it was delicious, and he ate it up greedily, talking about Sarah Wakefield's insulin.

'Though it's hopeless, really, to imagine we've got her

on the right dosage if her mother isn't capable of seeing that she eats the right amount of food at the right time.'

'I know. I'm pretty sure that's where the trouble lies.'

'She seems a nice enough woman, and fairly sensible.'

'I think she is. But she has no sense of time, and then, fundamentally, I suspect she's an egotist. Her marriage has gone bust, she's chasing a new boyfriend, and she's said to be depressed and moody.'

'She sounds like a recipe for an early death for the kid.'

'That's what I'm afraid of. That's really why I wanted Sarah in – to make her mother realize the seriousness of the situation, and so that we can hammer her about the importance of diet and routine.'

'And have you?'

'Hammered her? Oh yes. I got Walter to have a go, in the most heavy-handed manner possible – '

'Which is saying something.'

'Indeed, yes. And she's already seen the dietician twice, and I asked her to make heavy weather, so she tells me she is preparing new diet sheets, and a new list of exchanges, all in co-operation with Mrs Wakefield.' Caroline was anxious to have Sarah sorted out, and she was grateful to Daniel for giving his full attention to her in this way. But she wished he would let up for a bit, and allow her a chance to savour, not only the delicious meal, but also the bliss of knowing that she was alone with him at last.

But he didn't pause for a second. He seemed obsessed, this evening, by Sarah. Odd, that. He seemed, too, tense, on edge, unlike himself.

At last she cottoned on. Daniel was making it plain that this was a purely professional engagement, making sure that she didn't go away with the wrong idea, imagine that he'd taken her out because he was interested in her. That was what he was at. Hell, he needn't suppose she was some sort of nymphomaniac, non-stop on the catch for a man. In any case, if it came to that, she'd caught her man.

Except that all she could think about was how to ditch him.

No doubt about it, either, sitting here with Daniel while he went on about delayed-action insulin in a rapid almost machine-gun rattle was a world away from sitting opposite Jeremy, kind and reliable as he was. This was her world. She'd have to summon up her courage and tell Jeremy their engagement had been a mistake. Why had she allowed herself to get into such a false position?

They drank coffee, while Daniel made a sudden transition from soluble insulin to oral hypoglycaemic drugs, and looked almost wildly across at Caroline, his eyes all at once speaking a language that his lips denied. Caroline was startled out of her wits, but before she could pull herself together and make any sort of response, he had called for the bill.

He paid it, and they were on their way out. What might have happened next between them she was not to discover, for as they left, walking through the bar with its potted plants, they almost fell over Jeremy, sitting there with the blonde dietician, Fenella Jamieson. Both parties were taken aback, and Jeremy most of all. He looked, Caroline thought – almost with compassion – like a small boy caught in the act of raiding the refrigerator.

'Oh,' he uttered, his jaw dropping. He put his glass down on the table with a thud, and heads turned at the sound. 'Oh. Er – hello, Caroline. Daniel. Yes. Um. You know – er – Fenella?'

'Yes, we both know Fenella.' Daniel's eyes were alight with amusement. 'How are you, Fenella? Don't think I've seen you since – let me see – would it have been yesterday morning?'

Fenella, highly embarrassed, thought he was right. She

drank half a glass of gin and tonic in one gulp, and looked uncertainly at Jeremy.

'Can recommend the food,' Daniel said heartily. 'You'll enjoy it. Won't they, Caro?'

'Yes, I'm sure they will.' Caroline, who was beginning to enjoy herself, her morale raised astonishingly by the mere fact that Daniel had called her Caro again, as he had done years ago, wondered what would happen if she handed her ring back to Jeremy on the spot.

Daniel, however, gave her no opportunity to execute this dramatic gesture, instead hustling her away with his arm round her and a series of phrases about night rounds and being on call, until somehow they found themselves on the pavement outside the restaurant.

'Well,' Caroline exploded.

'Dare say he'll have an explanation,' Daniel suggested – Caroline never guessed how much the suggestion cost him.

As usual, too, he was right. At lunch the next day, Jeremy came through on the line, and caught her outside the ward, surrounded by a gaggle of students waiting to see her do a lumbar puncture. 'I hope you didn't get the wrong idea about last night,' he began cautiously. 'There was nothing in it, of course. I mean, not what you might have thought.'

'And what do you suppose I might have thought?' Caroline enquired dangerously.

'Well, after all, you know, I suppose it must have looked rather – rather – um – as if, you know, I – not that I for a moment intended any – um – still, it must have seemed rather as if . . .' He trailed miserably into silence.

'As if what?'

'Anyway, I can explain completely. There's not the slightest – look, I really can't go into it now, but how about meeting? And I'll tell you all about it. Tomorrow evening any good?'

Since Caroline couldn't see herself breaking her engagement in public view, on the wall telephone, surrounded by the students, her houseman, a staff nurse and two first-year nurses, all agog for every syllable that fell from her lips, she agreed to meet him at the flat the next evening, and put the telephone down. 'Right,' she said crisply to the assembly. 'Sorry to keep you all. Now, the indications for lumbar puncture are – what?'

Someone duly came up with them, there was some discussion, and the little group then proceeded into the ward, where Caroline and her houseman demonstrated the technique.

The following evening, though, everything went wrong. Caroline reached the flat in good time, but almost immediately she was recalled to the ward for a child with a rocketing temperature. She returned to find Jeremy on the doorstep, waiting for her in what appeared to be extreme irritation, though in fact he was eaten up with nerves, his condition in no way improved by hanging around on the stairs waiting for her. Taking Fenella out – in a good cause, too, so his conscience should have been clear – had seemed like fun. But now he had to pay the price – was this what married life was going to be like?

'Sorry to be late,' Caroline apologized. 'Have you been here long?'

'About ten minutes,' Jeremy told her, in distinctly huffy tones. This was not the way he had intended to start the evening, but he couldn't stop himself.

'Oh dear.' Caroline was put out. 'Come on in and have a drink, anyway.'

'There isn't much time. I've booked a table. I thought you'd be ready.' He glanced pointedly at his watch.

'Oh, have you?' She was dismayed. She'd been hoping they could have a quiet talk in the flat – the idea of going out to an expensive restaurant for the purpose of breaking her engagement filled her with horror. 'Couldn't we simply have our talk here, not go anywhere?' she suggested, but without much hope. Once Jeremy was embarked on a course of action, he was usually impossible to divert.

Tonight he was determined to take her out. It was, he'd decided, the least he could do. He owed it to her, after taking Fenella to the Country Garden – and who'd have dreamt he'd have run into Caroline there? He'd supposed her to be safely in the flat with Ginny and Robert.

Caroline gave in, though her heart sank. 'I'll change, then,' she said. 'I'll be as quick as I can.' She put on the easiest outfit she could lay her hands on, her old patterned velvet with a plain polo-neck and her mother's pearls, topped by her velvet jacket that she wore everywhere. Glancing hastily in the glass before she left, she decided that she looked everyone's idea of the clever young woman doctor, and no one's notion of a seductive girlfriend. Her heart sank, though she was at a loss to understand why – after all, if Jeremy looked at her and remembered two nights earlier and the fantastic Fenella with longing, that was exactly what she wanted to happen.

This way out.

If only she didn't carry this appalling load of guilt. Jeremy had been so supportive during her Stonebridge years, had helped her so much when she'd been in need. She herself was to blame for the situation, for having mistaken her feeling for him – lukewarm, she recognized now, compared with her overpowering emotion for Daniel. She should never have gone against her instinct, which had clearly warned her against involving herself permanently.

The restaurant he took her to was far grander than

the Country Garden, with teams of obsequious waiters, crimson velvet everywhere they turned, chandeliers and ankle-hugging carpet.

The meal, understandably, was not a success. The food was excellent, but it was eaten by two distracted individuals, an accompaniment to Caroline's apologies for ever having agreed to an engagement in the first place, and Jeremy's apologies for having taken Fenella out, coupled with a somewhat irritable demand to her not to take offence about nothing. Waiters and dishes came and went, while Caroline felt steadily more desperate – and guilt-ridden – and Jeremy more martyred and misunderstood.

'Of course I admit she's damned attractive, and I'm not pretending for a minute that I didn't enjoy taking her out, but it was for a very sound reason. When I met her at that party, you see, she told me her father was a chartered accountant, here in London. So if I wanted a job – '

Worse and worse. He'd contemplated pulling himself up by the roots, and all for her. 'But, Jeremy, that would mean leaving Stonebridge.' And what on earth would her father say, if Jeremy wanted to dissolve the partnership? 'You can't possibly be thinking – '

'We can keep our options open,' he said. 'You may decide you want to go on living near the Central for quite a while.'

This was terrible. 'It's sweet of you to think of moving on my account, but you mustn't change your job for me. And it's no good anyway, we aren't going to get married, you must understand I really do mean it. I'm so terribly sorry, it's all my fault. I should never have . . .' she was hauling frantically at the ring, but her hands were hot and sticky, and it refused to budge.

'Now wait a minute, Caroline. Look, you can't be serious – I keep telling you, Fenella meant precisely – '

'It's nothing to do with Fenella. It's simply that – oh, Jeremy, I'm so sorry. I'm terribly fond of you, but it isn't enough. You've been marvellous.'

'But *why*, suddenly, then? If it isn't Fenella?'

'I've tried to explain. It's really that I don't want to get married.' At last the ring came off her finger, and she handed it across the table. 'Please have this back now, Jeremy, and believe me that our engagement was a mistake. A mistake I made because I'm so fond of you. And grateful to you for all your support.' She sounded like the most pompous sort of chairman at the annual meeting. 'But it wouldn't work. And anyway I don't want to get married. I'm sorry. I should have said this much sooner.'

He eyed the ring as if it would bite him. 'I'm not taking that back.' Taking her decision seriously at last, and panicking, he sounded furious with her. Noticing this, he changed key. 'You must be overtired,' he told her gently. 'The new job being a bit much, eh? We – we'll postpone everything, have another talk when you're less tired. Put your ring on, and – and have a brandy.' That was the answer. He clicked his fingers for the waiter, who had been glued to the little scene, and came with alacrity. Jeremy ordered brandy, and pushed the ring surreptitiously back along the tablecloth towards Caroline. 'Put it on,' he hissed. 'People are beginning to notice.' He cast an angry glance round the restaurant, and a number of eyes switched direction.

The brandies arrived.

'Get that down you, and you'll feel better,' he said.

'I feel perfectly all right,' Caroline said angrily. 'And I don't need any brandy, thank you. But I would like you to look after your ring. We're no longer engaged. That's final. I hope we shall always remain friends. I'm very fond of you.' How ridiculous she sounded. What was more, she was making a scene in public. She'd do best to leave at once, before it got any worse. 'Thank you for everything,' she said, rising, picking up her bag and jacket, and turning away.

What seemed like a score of waiters materialized and helped her into the jacket.

'Madam's brandy?' one of them enquired tenderly.

'No, thank you.' Caroline swung on her heel, afraid one of them was going to say 'Madam's ring?' Her nose in the air, her expression calm and composed – being made a fool of on countless ward rounds over the years as a student and houseman turned out to have unexpected uses – she trod in a stately manner out of the restaurant, and out, she prayed, of Jeremy's life. She was free.

She'd seldom felt more awful. How horrible she'd been. But at least it was ended.

It should never have begun.

Sarah Leaves the Central

In the department they noticed at once, and it flew round the grapevine. Dr Milne had broken off her engagement. She wasn't wearing that enormous diamond. It was neither pinned to her lapel nor on her finger.

Several of them could provide the reason. Fenella Jamieson. That good-looking accountant who'd been engaged to Dr Milne had taken one glance at Fenella – at the departmental party in Daniel Harcourt's flat – and fallen for her. He'd taken her out to dinner two nights later. Several people had seen them together at the Country Garden – half the Central had been going there, since Paul Goddard had talked about it. And according to Paul, Daniel Harcourt had been there the same evening, with Dr Milne.

Daniel was the only individual to investigate the authenticity of this account. After a particularly gruelling ward round with his own chief, when Sir Graham had been more than usually pedantic, and had done his far from inadequate best to make mincemeat of them all, he demanded, as severely as the professor might have done, and like him out of the blue, 'Have you broken off your engagement to Jerrikins, Caro?'

Caroline, who was engaged in a rapid recapitulation of the round and the patients in her mind, checking over what points she had to follow up with whom, came out of this briefly, and said somewhat vaguely. 'My engagement? Broken it off? Well, yes, I have, that's right. And I do wish you wouldn't keep calling me that.'

Daniel was astonished. 'They can't have got it right. Do you mean to stand there and tell me you've broken it off simply because of that twit Fenella?'

'Fenella? Oh no, not Fenella,' Caroline said absently, as they went downstairs together. 'Oh no, it wasn't anything to do with her.'

'Why, then?'

Caroline looked at him for the first time, and he saw he had her whole attention at last. She was in fact asking herself what would happen if she said, 'Because of you.' But it was unthinkable. 'Oh,' she said evasively. 'It's a long story. Some other time, shall we?'

'No we shan't. Here and now.' He stopped on the next landing, stood foursquare in front of her, and said, 'Tell me at once. Tell me exactly why.'

'This is neither the time nor the place.' Caroline threw a hunted glance upstairs and downstairs.

'All right. Tomorrow, then. Let's go for a walk, and then have lunch somewhere.'

'I'm afraid my father and Ginny are up for the weekend. I'm awfully sorry. And anyway, I'm on call.'

'Tonight, then. We'll have a meal.'

'Well, I ought to –'

'Don't dare tell me you've got to stay in and cook for your father's arrival.'

Caroline laughed. Suddenly everything was fun again. 'I wasn't going to,' she said. 'Ginny does the catering when they come up. I'd love to have a meal.'

Daniel, too, found he was immensely pleased with life. 'Let's go somewhere where we don't meet half the hospital,' he suggested. 'That rules out Giovanni's and the Country Garden. Tell you what, let's go for a walk and drop in at a likely pub for a snack at the bar.'

'Super.'

'Shall I call for you?'

'Lovely. Say nine o'clock, to be on the safe side?'

'See you then.'

The London streets were once more carpeted with magic, and Caroline trod them with all the buoyancy she'd thought left behind for ever. It wasn't, either, that they did anything special – it was enough that they were together again, and she knew herself free. The uneasy feeling that she had become involved in something inescapable and unwanted had left her, as she told Daniel when he asked about her broken engagement. 'That was all it was,' she said. 'Simply a mistake that should never have happened. A mistake I should never have made, that wasn't fair to Jeremy. I only made it because he'd been so kind and such a support while I was at home, and I suppose I was grateful, and so I made this mistake. I knew as soon as I'd agreed to marry him that there was something wrong about it, that I wasn't ready to go through with it. But I kept putting off telling him so, because he was being so nice, and I *am* so fond of him. And it was difficult, too, because my father was so keen we should marry.'

They were eating hot sausages and French bread, and drinking Watney's Red Barrel, at a small public house known to most paediatricians, as it was a step or two down the road from the Hospital for Sick Children in Great Ormond Street. Daniel looked at her, and his glance burnt into her. He pushed his chair back. 'Thank God you're free of him,' he said. 'I didn't know how to bear it. Let's go.'

'Let's.'

'Your flat or mine?' he demanded, exactly as he'd done two years earlier.

'Doesn't matter.' Caroline was too happy to think, or

she'd have remembered that her father and Ginny would be arriving for the weekend – had, in fact, already reached St Anne's Square and were comfortably installed in the sitting room when Caroline and Daniel, treading on air, strolled in.

'Oh, my God.' Daniel backed out into the hall fast. 'I won't interrupt,' he said. 'You'll want to talk to them. See you.' He was gone, and she heard the outside door bang behind him.

The following morning, ostensibly in order to be free for lunch with her father and Ginny, but in reality in the hope of setting eyes on Daniel, Caroline went over to the hospital immediately after breakfast.

In the ward, Sister Heslip, the weekend duty-sister, told her that Sarah Wakefield was upset. 'That mother of hers never turned up yesterday afternoon to visit her. Sarah was absolutely thrown, poor lamb. And she hasn't got back on an even keel yet.'

'No message from Mrs Wakefield?'

'Not a word. And there was that poor little kid watching out for her from lunchtime on.'

'Oh, how awful. That bloody woman – I could shake her.'

'I was wondering, Doctor, if you'd have time to have a word with Sarah? Because she does look on you as her special doctor – she tells everyone so.'

Caroline glanced at her watch. She hadn't a spare moment. 'I'll make time,' she said firmly.

Sarah was peaky and anxious, frowning, but her face changed and lighted up when she saw Caroline approaching.

'I hear Mum didn't come to see you yesterday?'

'No.' Sarah hesitated, clearly on the brink of adding to the bare negative.

'Are you anxious about her?' Caroline asked, realizing

that Sarah, far from suffering pangs of homesickness as they had been visualizing, might in reality be worried about how her mother was managing in the caravan on her own.

'Well, yes, I am rather,' she admitted, relieved to unburden herself. 'You see, she promised me she'd come, so I'm sure she must have meant to. But if she was on her own, and a bit lonely, you know, and when she woke up I wasn't there, so she didn't have to see about my injection or anything like that, she'd probably go to sleep again, or read in bed. And then she'd get too late, and she'd miss the bus, and it would be no good trying to come up and see me. And she'd be all on her own for the whole evening. And she hates that.'

Caroline saw vividly the demands that daily life with Mrs Wakefield made on Sarah. However, she also saw that this dismal picture Sarah had painted for herself might exist only in her loving imagination. Far more likely that Mrs Wakefield had decided to have a day – and very likely night, too – with Mr Alsop. She was searching in her mind for suitable phrases in which to impart this alternative view to Sarah when her name was called, and one of the student nurses came quickly along the ward.

'Dr Milne, Dr Berkeley is asking for you on the telephone.'

'I'll come. Back in a minute, Sarah.'

She wasn't, though. Dr Berkeley was ringing from a patient's house, where he'd been called in by the family doctor. He'd found a child in status asthmaticus, and wanted him admitted within the hour. Caroline was involved in a spate of telephoning to arrange this, a discussion with Sister Heslip about discharges, and a trip down to Casualty to receive the severely ill, panting boy. They worked on him down in Casualty for an hour before they were able even to get him up to the ward, and it was another hour before Caroline could leave him and return to the flat, late for lunch. So far she'd hardly seen her father and Ginny, except for half an hour before bed the previous evening, and ten minutes at breakfast that morning. Immediately after lunch, too, she'd have to go back to the ward to have another look at the little asthmatic. She'd have to see Sarah at the same time, and discover whether Mrs Wakefield had appeared for today's visiting period, or whether, once again, she'd failed to show up.

Over a glass of sherry before lunch her father was mildly offended, saying that he'd hoped the hospital could have spared her for half an hour that morning to talk to her decrepit old father. He wanted, he added ominously, to have a little chat with her about her marriage plans.

'I haven't any,' Caroline said shortly.

That, her father said, was what he wanted to talk about. Jeremy had told him –

'Jeremy and I aren't going to get married, Dad. I told you. It was a mistake.'

'Are you sure it was?'

'Certain.'

'I suppose Stonebridge must seem rather dull to you. But you may not always feel like this, my dear. One day you may wish –'

Ginny called them to the table, and asked Robert to carve, while she started on an animated account of their visit to the ballet the previous evening. This carried them through the meal, when, leaving him to the Sunday papers, she and Caroline went off to the kitchen together to see to the washing up and brew coffee.

Ginny was apologetic but firm. 'I wasn't going to let him argue all through lunch,' she said, 'but I'm afraid Robbie is determined to have it out with you about breaking your engagement. He's rather upset about it. He had set his heart on you marrying Jeremy and both of you living in Stonebridge for ever. And then, of course, he is very fond of Jeremy, and wanted him for a son in-law. I've tried to get it across to him that he can't expect you to marry just to suit him, and to mind his own business. But of course he says it is his business, that he mustn't stand by and watch you throw away your future without protest. So you'll have to face it, and have it out with him this afternoon. I'll take myself off – but do try and remember, however maddening he is, it is all because he loves you so much.'

Caroline swished hot water and detergent round the washing-up bowl, and clattered knives and forks crossly. 'Well, it *is* my business and not his,' she said. 'And he'll have to accept it. I'm not marrying Jeremy just to keep him happy.'

'Of course not. You're quite right to lead your own life – and, personally, I never thought you and Jeremy were all that well suited. Robbie'll come round. The trouble is, he doesn't like the empty house, and in his imagination he's been seeing you and Jeremy raising a family there. But I've got an idea about the house, which ought to make quite a difference, I think. It's what I really wanted to discuss with you this weekend. I've a plan to make a really nice flat up in the attics, and offer it to Alan Peterson and his wife, with a slice of garden thrown in, plus the back lobby and the old pantries, and your mother's old consulting room, downstairs. So that he could see patients, I mean. That should bring the house to life again without involving you or Jeremy.'

Caroline, drying her hands, stared at Ginny. 'That's a super plan,' she said. 'How clever of you.'

Ginny gave her a straight look. 'Your father thinks – *hopes* would be more accurate – that you won't be in favour of it. He says we ought to keep the attics for a flat for you – with or without Jeremy, I may say.'

Caroline shook her head. 'No, I'd far sooner come and stay with you and Dad, and keep my old room, if that's OK with you. Or did you want it to turn into a sauna, perhaps, or an office to run your interior decoration firm from, when you've completed the Burvale alterations and begun on the rest of Stonebridge?'

'Neither. It's yours in perpetuity.'

They smiled at one another, their understanding complete, while the aroma of coffee filled the kitchen.

The telephone rang.

'Oh blast. Just when coffee's ready, too, wouldn't you know? You take it through, Ginny, and pour yours. I may have to go across to the hospital – if so Dad will have to defer his homily.' She answered the telephone.

Sister Heslip. They couldn't find Sarah Wakefield, and she thought Dr Milne would want to know.

'Do you mean she's not in the hospital?'

'It would seem not, Doctor. I've had my nurses out looking for her, and there's no sign. She's not to be found in any of the likely places.'

'Have you tried – ' Caroline began, but pulled herself up. 'Yes, of course you have. Silly of me. Did her mother – '

'Her mother hasn't appeared so far, and it *is* quite late, though I suppose she could be on her way still, if she's as unpunctual as Sarah makes out. But that was my first thought, that Sarah was down in the hall, or at the foot of the stairs, somewhere like that, hanging about waiting for her. But she's not to be seen.'

'Oh dear. I was coming over to see her this afternoon, too. If only she'd waited a bit – do you think she's panicked and set off for home?'

'It's what's in my mind, Doctor. I may be wrong, but – '

'I doubt it, Sister. It's in both our minds. Look, you go on hunting for her in the hospital, and in the meantime I'll get in the car and drive down to Waterloo, on the off-chance of picking her up there. She might be on the Stonebridge platform, if I'm quick.' She looked at her watch. 'The trains are only two-hourly – I might just make it.'

'Oh, if you would, Doctor. That would be a load off my mind. It's a long way for her to go on her own – '

Caroline thought of the Sunday evening wait for a bus out to the caravan site. Sarah might easily have a four-hour journey.

' – and she had her lunch at midday. She's due for another snack quite soon.'

'On my way, Sister.' Caroline put the telephone down, and then, on second thoughts, picked it up and rang Daniel. Luckily he answered on the second ring. She said, 'I've to drive to Waterloo, stat. Can you come with me? I'll explain on the way.'

'Car outside your block?'

'Yes.'

'Consider me there.'

He was as good as his word, and she was able to tell him about Sarah as they drove along the empty Sunday afternoon roads. 'The thing is, I need to dump the car and gallop for the Stonebridge platform. So if you could stay with it, while I hunt for Sarah – '

'Sure.'

'I'm so sorry to drag you out like this on a free Sunday,' she said. 'I have my father and Ginny with me, too, and one of them could easily have looked after the car, but I knew I'd only waste time arguing with my father as to whether I ought to set off at all, so I simply left them having coffee, rang you and walked out.'

'Sensible,' was all he said, though inwardly he was

extraordinarily pleased that she'd turned at once to him.

'Just get out and leave the car with me,' Daniel told her when they reached the station. 'I'll be somewhere around here. And good luck.'

Caroline ran through the ticket offices and across to the Stonebridge platform, still, she was thankful to see, scattered with travellers, the train not yet in. Hastily she explained her purpose to the ticket-collector at the barrier.

'Yes,' he said. 'There was a little girl on her own. I was a bit surprised. But she had her return ticket and said she was going home, so I didn't stop her. Sorry, Doctor. Wish I had now. You go right through.'

Halfway down the platform Caroline spotted her, standing alone and looking thoroughly miserable, in her blue anorak and her pyjama trousers – indistinguishable from blue jeans to a casual glance – and her sandals.

She was pleased to see Caroline, no doubt about it. She rushed at her and clung tightly to her. 'Oh, Dr Milne,' she exclaimed joyously. 'Oh, I was just wishing – are you going to Stonebridge too?'

'No. I was looking for you, you dreadful child. I hoped you'd be here, and took a chance – I was coming to see you in the ward this afternoon, you see, but they said you'd taken off for parts unknown.'

Sarah looked stricken. 'I should have waited, I know,' she admitted. 'I did wonder if you'd come back. But then I remembered it was Sunday afternoon, and I thought I oughtn't to bother you anyway. So I decided to go and see for myself if Mum was all right.'

'Yes, that's what I guessed you must be doing.'

'I suppose – I suppose really I ought not to have gone like that.'

Caroline gave her a quick hug. 'You should not,' she said. 'You most certainly should not. But I know how you felt. We'd better go back now, though, and make our peace with Sister Heslip.'

'Is – is she very cross?'

'A bit. But we'll go back and explain, and she'll understand, I'm sure. And I'll ring up Dr Peterson at the Hollies and get him to go out to the caravan and see how your mother is.'

'Oh, would you? Oh, thank you. I knew it would be all right if I asked you. I needn't have come here at all.'

'Come on, we'll go back now. Dr Harcourt is waiting for us in the car.'

'Dr Harcourt, too.' Sarah was impressed.

They were walking briskly along the platform now, towards the entrance. Caroline nodded to the ticket collector and thanked him, and then, holding on to Sarah's hand, set off across the wide concourse. 'We do both wish you'd stopped to consult us, though, Sarah. Because, for one thing, there's your next meal, and –'

'Oh, that would have been all right, Doctor. I've got biscuits and sugar in my pocket. I'd have eaten them in the train – I thought about that.'

'I see. It's not ideal, you know.'

'No. It was just that –'

'That you were so worried about Mum. I know. And as soon as we're back, I'll ring Dr Peterson, I promise.'

The Rover drew up to the kerb alongside them as they approached, Daniel at the wheel. 'Hi,' he said. 'Well done. Would you like to drive back?'

'No, you carry on, if you don't mind. Easier.'

'Right.'

'Come on, Sarah, you and I can both hop in the front and you can sit on my knee. We seem to be blocking the taxi rank.'

Driving back across Waterloo Bridge in the afternoon sun, the river sparkling below and the dome of St Paul's catching the light against the sky, Daniel demanded, 'And so what was the trouble, Sarah?'

'I was worried about Mum.'

'You could have told us.'

'Yes. I know I should have done. I nearly did, but then – then I remembered it was Sunday, you see, and I thought I ought to be able to manage on my own and not bother anyone.'

Daniel negotiated the traffic lights at the Strand and the turn into the Aldwych before replying. Then, as they sped up Kingsway in the big old car, he said 'You never have to manage on your own, Sarah. You must get that into your head. There's a whole hospital of people to help you. You must try and get into the habit of asking for help – or advice – when you need it.'

Caroline could feel the small body tense on her knee. She put her arms round Sarah and patted her shoulder. 'I know you meant it for the best,' she said. 'And I do understand why you felt you had to do something about your mother, I'd have been the same?'

'*You* would?' Sarah was taken by surprise.

'Oh yes, she would,' Daniel rejoined at once. 'She's a great one for going it alone, is our Dr Milne.'

'I don't think I – ' Caroline began indignantly.

'Oh yes, you do.' He interrupted her. 'Take all the responsibilities of the world on your inadequate shoulders, you would, without a word to a soul. You and Sarah are as bad as each other. Two of a kind.'

Sarah perked up at this. For Dr Harcourt to bracket her with Dr Milne made her day. Daniel waited for the traffic lights at Russell Square, and said 'Both of you could do with asking for advice more often. Take this afternoon, now.'

'Oh, I know about that,' Sarah said. 'Dr Milne told me. If I'd just waited, she would have come to see me.'

'And what I would have said is that Mum might not actually even be on her own in the caravan. She might be out with Mr Alsop for the day.'

'Oh, do you think so? I never thought of that. That would be super.'

'There you are, you see,' Daniel said. 'The value of consultation. Both of you take note.'

Through the quiet squares, they drove back to the Central together.

12

Complications

At teatime, Caroline, already feeling she had had more than enough of humanity and its foibles, went back to the flat, where having handled all the temperaments around the hospital with unshakable calm, she promptly flew off the handle as soon as her father began pressing her not to end her engagement.

'If you'd only listen to my advice,' Robert repeated, for what seemed to Caroline the ninety-ninth occasion.

'I am listening to it. I've done nothing else since I came in.'

'No need to jump down my throat, my dear.'

'Sorry. But –'

'No need to apologize, either. I know what it is. You're worn out.'

This was the exact truth, but Caroline refused to accept it. 'I'm perfectly all right,' she asserted irritably.

'You're run off your feet all day long, as well as short of sleep. And it's interfering with your judgement. That's why I'm asking you at least to defer any final decision about your engagement. Jeremy will understand.'

'I don't need him to understand. It's finished.'

'If you'd only wait, let things ride for a while. I don't like to see you throwing away your chances of a happy marriage like this.'

'I'm not throwing away anything,' Caroline blazed. She ignored Ginny's warning gestures – she'd come in with the tea things in an attempt to break up the session before it ended in a flaming row. But she was too late. Caroline had lost her temper. 'I'm in love with someone else,' she yelled angrily at her father. 'So how the hell can I be engaged to Jeremy? Can't you see I'm in a completely false position unless I break it off?' She had lost control. Too late, she caught her breath, and would have recalled the words if she had been able to.

'In love with someone else? What on earth do you mean, my dear? How can you be? With whom?' Her father was shaken to the core.

So was Ginny. 'Who with?' she demanded excitedly.

'Who?' Caroline floundered. She must say nothing more. Already she'd said far too much, and it was all going to be hideously awkward. 'Daniel Harcourt,' she heard herself announce with clarity, adding for good measure 'and what's more, I'm going to marry him.' Just in time, she bit back the childish 'so there' that had almost popped out.

Two stupefied voices repeated 'Daniel Harcourt?'

'You can't marry *him*.' Robert, now as upset as Caroline, blundered badly. 'You haven't met him, Ginny,' he added, making bad worse. 'He came to stay for the weekend once, and I can't say I took to him. Clever enough – in his own line, I dare say, but an opinionated young man. Ungroomed, too. Dreadful suit.'

'Clever *enough*.' Caroline sizzled. The final straw. 'He's brilliant, that's all,' she rapped out. 'And you may have found him what you call opinionated – I suppose you mean a bit argumentative – but I can tell you he's straight, and honest and true right through to the core, even if his tailor doesn't happen to be the same as yours and Jeremy's.' At this stage, to her annoyance, she burst into tears, thus fully endorsing her father's earlier remarks.

He patted her shoulder kindly, and nodded at Ginny. 'Just as I said,' his glance meant. 'Overwrought.' Aloud he said only, 'A cup of tea, my dear, and I dare say you'll feel a good deal better.'

Ginny poured tea, and she and Robert began to cosset Caroline as though she'd been a miserable two-year-old until the time came for them to leave for the Stonebridge train.

Caroline took the tea tray out to the kitchen when they'd gone, and washed up. What could have come over her? She should have said nothing, or at least have withdrawn what she'd said about marrying Daniel. Suppose he found out what she'd said? She caught her breath at the possibility.

Nonsense, he'd never know. She'd simply had a family upset, and no one would ever hear anything about it. Furious with herself still, she pushed the affair to the back of her mind, and went across to the hospital to look at Dr Berkeley's asthmatic boy, who, to her relief, she found improved.

On her way back she was called to the telephone. Alan Peterson, to say that there'd been no sign of Mrs Wakefield at the caravan, but that he had spoken to the site warden, who had expressed himself as unsurprised that Sarah remained unvisited, saying that since her admission to hospital Mrs Wakefield had hardly spent five minutes together at the caravan. 'Out with that boyfriend of hers,' he'd explained. 'Sleeping over at his place, too.'

'Yes,' Caroline said. 'That's rather what I imagined. Thanks, Alan. It was good of you to go out there. I'll go along now and put Sarah's mind at rest. She thought something awful might have happened to her mother.' She rang off, and went along to see Sarah. She found Daniel there, allowing her to defeat him at draughts.

'Oh,' Caroline said. 'You're here. I wanted to have a word with you, anyway.' But how on earth was she going to explain what she'd said? What was there she could say?

'Sure.' He was easy. 'I've been well and truly beaten, so I'm on my way out with my tail between my legs.'

Sarah, shining with triumph, giggled happily.

'Dr Peterson rang,' Caroline told her. 'He went along to the caravan, but your mother wasn't there. So he spoke to the warden –'

'Mr Denman, that would be.'

'Yes. And he said she was out with Mr Alsop.'

'Oh, *good*.' Sarah appeared to mean this. 'That's all right, then.'

'Yes. Mr Denman said your mother has been spending a lot of time with Mr Alsop since you've been in hospital.'

'Oh well, that's a relief.' Sarah sounded fifty if a day. 'I needn't worry any more, then. I dare say they'll get married. It was very kind of Dr Peterson to go round and find out.'

'Yes, it was.'

'I expect Dr Milne twisted him round her little finger,' Daniel explained to Sarah, getting to his feet and stretching. 'That would be it.'

'Would it?' Sarah was interested.

'She does it to all of us,' Daniel told her.

'Oh, don't be so ridiculous,' Caroline said, annoyed to find herself blushing, and wishing that she could only succeed in dealing with Daniel in the way he suggested.

They said good night to Sarah and walked back along the ward together.

'Something on your mind?' he asked.

'Well, yes, there is, as a matter of fact.' How did he know? In any case, it didn't matter, because she would be torn in pieces before she breathed a syllable of it in his direction.

'Tell Uncle.'

If only she could. But he was the last person. Hell, no, they knew each other, she could tell Daniel anything, and it would be a relief to get it off her chest. 'Well, I – the fact is, Daniel, I – you're going to think I'm an awful fool, but – it was my father, you see. He said – and the thing was, I – '

'Ah, there you are, Caroline. They said I'd find you here. Just coming in to have another look at my new admission. They said you were ahead of me.'

Walter Berkeley.

'What did you make of him?'

Caroline cast a look of anguished desperation at Daniel, and began talking vehemently to Dr Berkeley about the little asthmatic boy.

In the cold light of the following morning, she was at a loss to understand her behaviour of the previous day. What in the world had possessed her? First the absurd scene with her father, and then, if it hadn't been for Dr Berkeley, she'd have blurted out the whole story to Daniel, of all people, the one person who must never discover that it was because of him that she'd broken her engagement. Madness to have told her father and Ginny, but Daniel ... She felt herself go scarlet at the thought, and her hand reached for the telephone. She'd ring Ginny and impress on her that she must on no account breathe a word about Daniel, and get her to see that her father's lips remained sealed.

However, there was no reply from Burvale. Caroline rang at intervals during the day, but the telephone rang on, unanswered, until the evening, when her father answered, at his most tetchy. 'What is it now, Caroline?' he enquired, in unloving accents. 'Ginny? No, I'm not going to interrupt her now, she's in the kitchen – we're having the Sneath-Robinsons for dinner, and she's busy.'

'Oh, I see. I'll ring her tomorrow,' Caroline said hastily. The Sneath-Robinsons were valued clients of her father's, over whom he was inclined to make an inordinate fuss. To try to explain anything to him with the Sneath-Robinsons in the offing would be a waste of time, and to drag Ginny away from the kitchen just then the height of selfishness. In any case, there wasn't any panic, after all, other than in her own mind. No one was going to confide to Daniel what she had said about him to her father and Ginny, two hundred miles from the Central, and leading their own lives.

The next day, with outpatients in the afternoon, would have been exceptionally busy even without Dr Berkeley's asthmatic. This little boy was considerably improved – or had been until his mother arrived and raised the roof with demands and accusations. Demands for Dr Berkeley in person, and accusations of incompetence, if not negligence, all round. Dr Berkeley refused to meet her, taking refuge in his house in St Anne's Passage, and intimating that he proposed to remain there until someone could inform him that she had left the hospital. It fell to Caroline to pacify her. She succeeded, but at the cost of a vast chunk of her already heavily committed time.

Around six in the evening, having missed lunch, and had only tepid tea and stale biscuits in outpatients, she decided to return to the flat for scrambled egg and coffee. On her way out of the ward, though, they told her that yet another problem mother was asking for her. Mrs Wakefield. 'She's in the ward, with Sarah, and she particularly wanted to talk to you as soon as you were free,' the staff nurse explained. 'She's rather upset – blaming herself for what happened on Sunday. She says she must see you.'

'Oh, all right.'

'Sister said to use the office.'

'Thanks very much.'

'I'll bring her along.'

Mrs Wakefield, flushed and apologetic, was contrite, and looking very pretty and appealing. 'Dr Milne, I'm so dreadfully sorry about what happened. Mr Denman told me about Dr Peterson coming to find me, and now Sarah says it was all because she was worried, and set off home.' Her eyes met Caroline's. 'I never thought she'd do anything like that,' she said. 'It's awful – if I'd had any idea how she was feeling – '

'She thought you were alone there, you see.' Caroline reminded herself forcefully that she was there to treat Sarah's diabetes, not to supervise Mrs Wakefield's private life. But the problem was – and it became plainer every day – that Mrs Wakefield's private life was what was wrong with Sarah.

'I was out with Mr Alsop,' Mrs Wakefield explained unwillingly, fiddling with the clasp of her bag – new and expensive, Caroline noted. Very likely, she decided uncharitably, a gift for favours received. 'He's on at me to marry him, you know.'

'And do you want to?'

'I suppose I would like to, really. I know it didn't work the first time, and a good deal of it was my fault. I can see that, looking back. But I've explained all about it to Clive – Mr Alsop, that is – and he says it won't happen again.'

Oh, won't it? 'And what do you think?'

'I'm no good on my own, Doctor, that's the trouble. I need someone – and at present it has to be Sarah, poor duck. It isn't fair to her, but as long as we're alone together, she's the one I depend on. And it isn't right.'

'I think it's quite a responsibility for a ten-year-old.' Caroline was gentle. Mrs Wakefield, quivering with nerves and guilt, had won her sympathy. And in any case, who was she, she wondered, to talk about what people should do? She'd become engaged to Jeremy, whom she knew now she'd never loved, because it was easy, and she was lonely. She was no better at arranging her life than Mrs Wakefield. She'd hurt Jeremy, just as Mrs Wakefield was hurting Sarah.

'I know. I didn't realize how much until Mr Denman told me about her being so worried, and then I asked her myself, just now, and – I know it must seem very silly and thoughtless of me, but it had never crossed my mind she would actually *worry* about me. I thought she'd understand. She knows how bad I am about catching trains, so I thought she'd assume I'd missed it, and that would be the end of it.'

'That was what she did think.' Caroline agreed. This was the moment. She had to place the truth squarely before Sarah's inefficient, well-meaning mother, somehow face her with the unavoidable facts so that she comprehended what was at stake, and did something about it. 'You know, we've had Sarah here for ten days now, and we've found nothing new. Yet she keeps going into coma. What must be happening is that when she's away from the hospital her meals and her insulin aren't matching up. Now, it does seem to me that this may be caused by what you've just been talking about – the fact that you aren't all that good on time-keeping. What do you think?'

'Oh, Doctor, I do try, really I do, but somehow, I don't know how it is, time seems to vanish.'

'It must be extra difficult in that small caravan, I do see that. It isn't truly the best place for a child like Sarah, I don't honestly think, do you?'

'No. No, it isn't. I used to think it would be perfect for her – out of the city, nice country air, and walks. But it's routine Sarah needs, I see that now. Her Dad would give her that – that was what used to get me down, him and his dreary old routine. Everything at the same time, day after day. My life was vanishing in week after week of meals at the right time, everything in order, dust and hoover and keep it neat and tidy for ever and ever until I was dead. It was a nightmare. I had to break out.'

'What about Mr Alsop?' Caroline could see Mrs Wakefield heading for the same problems over again. 'Won't he expect –'

'He's quite different.' Mrs Wakefield was confident. 'He works for himself – he has a greengrocery van, and he goes round the estates and the back streets. A new district each day. Long hours, he has to work, but every day is different. Like one day he's up at dawn to go to market, and then it's the afternoon round the Wates houses. Another day it'll be the Council estate, not starting before ten, but going on into the evening. Never the same two days running, and he says I can go with him in the van and help serve.'

Super for Mrs Wakefield, but a dead loss for Sarah. Less routine than ever. 'How would you fit Sarah in?'

'That's just it, Doctor. That's what's worrying me. It wouldn't be good for her, and anyway she wouldn't like it. She's one for routine, same as her dad.'

Caroline took the plunge. 'Would he have her to live with him?'

'Jump at it. Didn't like parting with her.'

'Then don't you think perhaps –'

'I love her too.' At once Mrs Wakefield was angry.

'I'm sure you do. But –'

'It's no good, Doctor. I can see it would be best for her, but I don't think I could do it. I'd miss her so.'

Caroline thought of the small indomitable Sarah, and understood. Plain, determined, feet on the ground, Sarah would not only be a comfort to come home to, but she had inherited from her mother something of that quality

156

of appeal, and she could encroach stealthily into the affections, so that even for Caroline, when she'd gone from the ward after a mere two-week stay, there'd be a gap, a feeling of someone missing. 'Yes,' she agreed. 'I can see it could be impossible to part with her.'

Mrs Wakefield dropped her air of challenge. 'I feel so split, Doctor, I don't know what to do. One day I decide one thing, and then the next morning, I know it's no good, and it's all off again. I'd like to marry Mr Alsop, but it does mean losing Sarah, and I don't think I could bear to.' Her face crumpled. 'We've always been so close, Sarah and me,' she said, and began to cry. 'I'm sorry, Doctor, but I don't think I could part with her. Only I don't want to lose Clive either. He — he's right for me. And I wouldn't know how to go on without him. Not now. But he's not going to hang around for ever, is he, waiting for me to make up my mind?'

'It looks to me, you know, as if you're going to have to face up to letting one of them go.' But did Mrs Wakefield ever face up to anything? More likely she drifted with the current, and went wherever it took her. And what was she doing herself, Caroline wondered? Drifting about ineffectively between her father and Jeremy. She'd only begun to take a stand during the past week. She had to stop trying to keep her father and Jeremy happy, find her own path, and walk steadily along it. With Daniel, if he wanted to accompany her. But without Jeremy. And independently of her father. And she didn't have to use Daniel to get out of marrying Jeremy, either. She should never have dragged his name into the argument, simply to hide behind. She had to remain firm, and follow her own path. Not her father's or Jeremy's, but her own.

As luck would have it, after she'd parted from Mrs Wakefield, she ran straight into Daniel, waiting for the lift. All her resolutions vanished, and suddenly the only thing she wanted was to come clean, to confide in him, unburden herself. He'd understand. 'Oh, Daniel,' she said. 'I was wanting to see you. I wanted to talk to you.'

They stepped into the lift, and he pressed the button for the ground floor. 'Got anything on?' he enquired. 'Or could we have a meal?'

'I'd love to.'

They came out of the lift, crossed the entrance hall, and set off across the car park. Caroline embarked on her confession. 'I must tell you,' she began. 'I've been an awful fool. I don't know what you're going to say, I've been such an idiot, but the thing was, I – ' Almost the same ominous opening, though she was unaware of it, that she'd offered him a few days earlier, and that he'd been worrying about steadily ever since.

At this moment, unluckily for them, they ran into Sir Graham, scrambling long-leggedly, like a trapped Daddy-Long-Legs, out of the white Mini – actually belonging to Lady Williamson – that he habitually used as a run-around between his home, Mortimer's and the Central.

'Ah,' he said. 'Good. I was coming in search of you, Daniel. I want to have another look at my fibrocystic girl. I've been thinking, maybe if we . . .'

Daniel, with a mouthed 'I'll ring you' to Caroline, turned and went back into the hospital with his chief, and Caroline went home alone, trying to convince herself that the interruption had been just as well. She really had no need to tell Daniel anything – what could have come over her recently? She seemed set on blurting out all the wrong things.

She couldn't be exactly easy in her mind, though, and she would have been even less easy if she'd been aware that Daniel had gone off confirmed in his impression that her engagement to Jeremy was on again.

13

In the Common Room

Sarah was discharged, and went home to Mrs Wakefield and the caravan. Caroline remained worried about her, but there seemed nothing more she could do, other than to ring the long-suffering Alan Peterson and impress on him the necessity of keeping in touch with the caravan at Edge Side. He assured her he'd be out there jet-propelled if Mrs Wakefield rang as an emergency, and with that Caroline had to be satisfied. She'd done what she could. She would have been enormously relieved if she'd known that her words to Mrs Wakefield had borne fruit.

Over a special meal, ostensibly to celebrate Sarah's return, she told her she was going to marry Mr Alsop. 'Now, we'd like you to come and live with us, of course. But we must face facts, there would be problems.'

'Not a man for a regular life, I'm not,' Mr Alsop explained. 'Out and about in the van at all hours, that's me. And I'd like your mum to come with me, see?'

'Yes.' Sarah tried to remain cool, but a great hope was starting to spread through her, and excitement rose. No more caravan and worrying about Mum? Off back to Dad and Sue and the new baby in Hemel Hempstead?

It was true. 'It isn't that I shan't miss you dreadfully, pet,' Mrs Wakefield told the blissful Sarah. 'I don't know how I'm going to manage without you. But it wouldn't be right, Dr Milne made me see that.'

Wonderful, super Dr Milne.

'You must come and stay, though. Often.'

'Of course. Lovely,' Sarah assured her conscientiously.

'You're sure it's all right?' her mother persisted. 'You truly don't mind?'

'I don't mind.' Sarah made the understatement of her short life without a tremor, and added, duty-bound, 'but I shall miss you, too.'

'So it's all right with you if I write off to your Dad?'

'Yes. Or I could write for you,' Sarah suggested, afraid that her mother would, as usual, procrastinate and the letter remain unwritten for weeks.

'No. I must write to him myself.'

So relentlessly did Sarah pursue the matter, though, that the letter was written and posted off within a few days. Saying nothing to Mrs Wakefield, Sarah sat down and wrote a full and detailed letter to her father, and another to Dr Milne, to whom she owed this happy state. The letter reached Caroline in the department office, and she skimmed through it hastily, saw it posed no worrying problem but seemed instead to be a joyous thank you, so put it into her pocket to read when she had a spare moment.

At lunchtime she went into the residents' common room for a coffee and sandwich – busy housemen and registrars rarely used the canteen for lunch. The cooking was excellent, but at midday it was packed, so that anyone who wanted a snack in fifteen minutes went to the common room instead, and snatched coffee and one of the sandwiches brought in from the delicatessen daily on a rota system. Today's contribution was cottage cheese and cucumber on brown bread provided by a conscientious cardiologist, and Caroline helped herself to the last but one, together with some lukewarm coffee, and sat down in the fast-emptying room – nearly two already, she saw with a shock – to read Sarah's letter. This told her a good deal more than its writer imagined. Mum and Mr Alsop were going to be married. Mr Alsop seemed able to manage Mum, who was very energetic and chatty, quite different from usual. But the real news was that she, Sarah, was going to live with Dad in Hemel Hempstead, and she wanted to thank Dr Milne for talking to Mum, because this was what had made it all happen. Next time she came to outpatients she expected Dad would come with her and Dr Milne could meet him. There was a PS : 'Thank you and Dr Harcourt for fetching me from the station that Sunday, and I will remember what he said.'

Caroline had been conscious for the last twenty seconds that Daniel was in the room. He poured himself the dregs of the coffee, took the last battered sandwich, and came and sat down next to her.

'Jerrikins?' he enquired nastily, seeing her absorbed in her letter.

'Heavens, no.' She was surprised. 'I told you that was all over.' She didn't look up, or she would have seen the relief flood his face. 'This is Sarah Wakefield.' She passed him the letter. 'She'll remember what you said.' Her long finger pointed to the postscript.

With an effort, Daniel pulled himself together, though happiness was whizzing about all over him, he felt, almost popping visibly out of every pore. But he sipped his horrible coffee and scanned the note. 'Poor brat,' he said. 'Sensible, though. Will probably make out.' His enunciation, through brown bread and cottage cheese, would have repelled Robert Milne.

Caroline drank in every syllable.

Daniel's dark eyes bored into her skull, in the disconcerting way they had. 'Why are you so involved with the kid?'

'Am I? I don't think I'm any more – ' She broke off. He was right. She had always been over much involved with Sarah. 'I suppose I identify with her a bit. I'm perfectly healthy, thank God, but otherwise we're awfully alike.'

'In what way?'

'Oh, I don't know. She's independent, and – '

'And responsible. You share that quality. Pointed it out to you that day we had her in the car.'

'I don't think I am specially responsible. Not more than average. But I know exactly how she feels about her mother and how Mrs Wakefield doesn't mean to let her down, but does. And what this does to Sarah. My mother was just the same.'

'Yours?' He stared. 'She can't have been. Your mother was a family doctor.' He sounded shocked.

'The effect was not unlike having Mrs Wakefield, though. All her patients came first, before me. And she was for ever promising to be there, and then not turning up. My father usually stood in for both of them. As a child, I adored him.'

'As a child? Not now?' He was on to it like a flash, and shot the enquiry at her.

'Well, I did find him very difficult to take during those two years I was at home – it was a reaction to losing Mother, I know, and I tried to make allowances, but I suppose I looked at him for the first time then with adult eyes.'

'That weekend I came down I thought you were fixated on him to the point of abnormality.' Daniel was short.

'He was afraid, you see, that you were going to entice me back to Central, and he'd be left alone in that miserable empty house. He's afraid of being alone.'

'In that house, I don't wonder. It scared me stiff.'

'*Scared* you?'

'Terrified me out of my wits.' He was grim.

She looked at him, and saw he was speaking the truth. 'You were feeling as upset as Dad,' she said, her eyes widening. 'And I never noticed. I simply thought you'd understand about him – how he was. It never struck me that you could possibly be feeling one down.'

'About ten down,' he said. 'I don't come from your sort of background, Caro, face it.' She'd got to damn well face it, he knew that now. He'd wasted two long heart-broken years trying to persuade himself that their back-grounds and families were hopelessly incompatible, and it hadn't come off.

'My sort of background?' She was blank.

'A great house. With a drive that takes two cars without even noticing, and a father like a headmaster.'

'Was that how you found him?'

He nodded.

'I never think of him like that. He's a shy man, you know. Not like my mother at all, who could talk to any-one. I'm much more like him underneath, but a bit like Mother on top, I suppose, because of having been reared in the middle of the practice, perhaps. But I'm always better with patients than with personal friends. Like Dad, I'm shy.' It cost her a good deal to force out this truth. 'I'm shy of you, often.'

He'd been watching her narrowly, dwelling on each flicker of expression that crossed her face, and he saw that what she said was true. Suddenly his viewpoint shifted, and instead of Dr Caroline Milne from the Central, cool and imperturbable, clever and unruffled, snobbish and even a bit grand, he saw a small vulnerable Caroline, brought up among a crowd of busy family doctors, but a bit left out and overwhelmed. And alongside the admiration and desire she'd aroused in him from the first moment he saw her, a new tenderness was born.

Another sensation impressed itself on him, too. An uneasy awareness that time had passed. Almost as though his arm were weighted with lead, so reluctant was he to confirm this impression, he dragged his wrist up to his unwilling eyes. 'Five *past*,' he announced incredulously. He stood up. 'I ought to have been in outpatients with the old man at two o'clock.' His voice remained disbelieving.

Caroline looked at her own watch, and, pointlessly, shook her wrist, as though this might cause time to run backwards for them.

'Hell.' He stood looking down at her.

She loved every centimetre of the lanky frame in the unpressed suit, with a love that, like his, pulsed with a new tenderness. All she said, prosaically, was 'Better break the sound barrier, stat.'

'Will do. See you. Seems to me you and I have wasted one hell of a lot of useful time.' He didn't kiss her. He didn't dare, fearing that if he did his watch might betray him by advancing another five or ten unrecorded minutes. Briefly, he fingered a straying lock of her dark hair, placed it very gently where it belonged. And still he couldn't bear to leave her.

'Go on. Or the prof will liquidate you.'

'Too right.' He went, at last, without a backward look, leaving Caroline bemused. She sat on in the deserted room for a full ten minutes, and then wandered up to the ward, where they found her most unusually vague. Sister asked her staff nurse if she thought Dr Milne could possibly have had a liquid lunch. 'Though it wouldn't be like her. And there was no smell on her breath. But she certainly wasn't herself.'

For the next week, Daniel rang her every morning at breakfast, and every night around midnight. They exchanged details of their day, and made plans to meet – other than at the bedside, or in the lecture hall. The plans came to nothing. This was because of the seminar on Management of the Growth-Retarded Child, running

164

throughout the week in the medical school's main lecture theatre, with ward rounds and demonstrations around the hospital thrown in.

As senior registrar to the department, Caroline was responsible for its proper running while all its shining lights were either presiding over or delivering lectures and demonstrations. She was not in any way aided by the fact that Walter Berkeley, who considered her his personal private property, resented the seminar – mainly because Sir Graham was its chairman, while he himself had merely been invited to give a teaching round – and did his best to prevent his own staff from going anywhere near the lecture theatre.

Sir Graham, on the other hand, expected her not only to attend all the lectures – or at least to know who had said what, and exactly how he, as chairman, had handled the discussion throughout – but to follow all teaching rounds and demonstrations and let him know how they went, while at the same time remaining with her finger metaphorically on the pulse of every seriously ill patient in the ward, ready to provide a run-down on their conditions at the drop of a hat. Since he expected roughly the same feat from Daniel, together with his constant presence at the bedside of patients deprived of the professor's own clinical care while he sat chairing the seminar, it was hardly surprising that Caroline and Daniel found their planned hours together extinguished.

The seminar at last over, Daniel had to take off at once for the midlands for his parents' silver wedding celebrations, which had had to be postponed on his account from their rightful date a week earlier.

Without him, Caroline found the hospital empty, while lacking his telephone calls early and late the flat was a desert. However, on the third day a letter came. 'I wish you were here,' he began. 'At least I don't, because it would be difficult and complicated, you'd never fit in, and you wouldn't enjoy it.' Her heart plummeted. 'My parents would be afraid of you, just as I was afraid of your father that awful weekend. But somehow you'll have to learn to understand them, and I'll have to learn to take your father. Because we belong together, you and I.' Caroline began to breathe again. 'We'd better join our lives, and start dealing with all that this entails soonest.'

'Hope you agree,' he added in uncharacteristically small and crabbed writing at the foot of the page, as he lost confidence. He'd stared out of his back window on to the yard, wondering how he could possibly bring her here, and then, as he thought about her, his confidence came surging back, with all the new tenderness for her welling up too. His Caro. His for ever. Clever, brilliant and beautiful. Also vulnerable, over-conscientious and far too eager to meet every demand that was made.

Home was not here any longer, not in this familiar old terrace, nor would it ever be in Burvale. Home was where Caro was. 'Home,' he wrote, in a hand that wasn't crabbed at all, but big and sprawling and legible again, 'home is where you are. All my love, D.'

14

Sarah Alone

This was the morning Sarah's dad was to collect her and take her Hemel Hempstead. She was far too excited to sleep on, and made her mother a cup of tea at the unwelcome hour of 6.30 a.m.

She and Mrs Wakefield did Sarah's last-minute packing. Most of her possessions had gone two days ago, in a trunk purchased by Mr Alsop, who now arrived, announcing his intention of taking Mrs Wakefield off for the afternoon, for a trip to the sea. 'Because she's bound to mope when you've left, Sarah love. And I don't want her mooning about here all day upsetting herself.'

'Why don't you go off now, and leave me here to meet Dad?' Sarah suggested eagerly.

'I don't think we'd better do that.'

'Why not?' Sarah saw herself playing hostess to her father in the caravan. 'Do go. Do take her off now. It'll be much easier for her. She won't like saying goodbye, and seeing me go off with Dad, you know she won't.'

Mr Alsop did know. But he was amazed to find Sarah was aware of it. Funny, unexpected little kid. He scratched his head and thought about it. 'I don't know,' he said. 'It doesn't seem right.'

'Of course it's perfectly all right. Come and tell Mum.' Sarah, who'd gone with him to the van to search for his cigarettes, dragged him back to Mrs Wakefield and informed her she was going to the sea for the day, and they were leaving *now*, 'I'll wait here for Dad.'

Mrs Wakefield protested. But she was relieved at the prospect of avoiding Sarah's father, an encounter she'd been dreading, and they soon talked her round to accepting the plan.

'Your father's arriving on the 12.45 train,' she reminded Sarah, who knew all the details by heart anyway. 'And he'll catch the one o'clock bus out here. He said he'd bring sandwiches, so you can make him a cup of coffee and be in good time for the 2.30 bus.'

Sarah was impatient. 'I know.'

'I wrote it all down for him.'

'I know.'

'Come on, don't stand about gabbing all morning. The kid knows what's what all right.'

'Are you sure you'll be OK, Sarah?' Mrs Wakefield persisted.

' 'Course. Why ever not?' Sarah was offhand.

'Come on, girl, hop in.'

So Mrs Wakefield hugged an unresponsive Sarah, and climbed into the van. At last they were off. Sarah waved dutifully, but she was really thinking about what she had to do. She'd use the best cups for coffee, the same as she'd done that day Dr Milne came to tea.

A shadow passed the window as she was setting the little table. Oh, he'd caught an earlier train. She rushed to the door. But it was only Mr Denman, the site warden.

'Hullo, young Sarah. Got a message for you. Your father rang up just now.

He wasn't coming.

'Can't he come after all?' Her lip trembled, though she willed it not to, and she knew Mr Denman saw she was upset.

'Oh yes, nothing to worry about. He's on his way.'

Sarah had been aware of her lip trembling, but she

168

had no notion of how transfigured she became at these beautiful words.

'He's going to be late, though. There's work on the line, he said, it being Sunday.'

'Oh, I see.' Sarah nodded wisely, though she had no real idea of what this meant.

'He rang to say he had to take the railway bus, and he thought he might not catch the train. So what he wants is for you and your mum to meet him at Waterloo. Where is she, by the way? I thought she was here with you.'

'No, she's gone to the sea with Mr Alsop.'

'You mean she's not coming back? I saw the van go, but I never supposed she was in it. I thought she was going to wait and see your dad.'

'Well, she was.' Sarah was collecting her belongings, reaching for her anorak. 'But we persuaded her not to. She'd only have got miserable. But it doesn't matter in the least. I can perfectly well go to Waterloo on my own.' She cast a last, hasty look round the caravan, helped herself to most of the money in the housekeeping purse for her fare – Mr Alsop would lend Mum some extra – and picked up her case.

'Go by yourself?' Mr Denman was nonplussed.

'Of course.'

Poor little scrap. Mr Denman was very angry, and not for the first time, with Mrs Wakefield. Imagine clearing off like that, leaving the kid on her own. 'I can't get in touch with your dad again, I don't think,' he said regretfully. 'To get him to come down and fetch you after all. He was ringing from the station, you see, waiting for the bus they'd put on. He'll be on it now, and then he was going to get the train, and then the underground to Waterloo, he said. He'd meet you in the usual cafeteria. Your mum would know the one.'

'I know exactly.' Sarah was firm. 'I shall be quite all

right, honestly, Mr Denman. I'm very good at looking after myself.'

And you need to be, he thought. Damned shame. 'I wish I could come with you myself,' he said. 'But I've got three or four couples coming to look over caravans for holiday lettings, so I don't see how I can push off. I'll see you on to the bus, though, if you're sure you're going to be able to manage for yourself at the station.'

'I'm used to going to Waterloo by train,' Sarah assured him. 'I've done it heaps of times.'

'Well, I don't care for it, and that's a fact. But I suppose it'll have to do.'

To Sarah's indignation, Mr Denman not only saw her on to the bus but told the driver to make sure she got the London train. As a result, Sarah, mortified and fuming, was passed from hand to hand like a baby – from the bus-driver to the ticket-collector, then to the porter, and finally, when the train came in, to the guard, who put her into a carriage with two kindly middle-aged ladies.

When the train arrived at Waterloo, she didn't wait for the guard to come and collect her, as he'd promised, but skipped out fast, and was through the barrier like a flash, in a rush to join her father, waiting for her in the familiar cafeteria.

He wasn't there.

At the Central, Caroline and Daniel were planning a free Sunday afternoon and evening, their first real time together since the seminar. They'd go for a walk, they decided, and afterwards they could have a meal in Caroline's flat before doing a late round. In the department it was reasonably quiet, for a change, and they asked Walter Berkeley's present registrar, Adrian Forsyth, to stand in for them while they got some air.

'Air?' he asked. 'What's that?'

'That stuff that blows about outside.' Daniel gestured widely. 'We thought we might breathe it for a couple of hours.'

'I'd be careful,' Adrian warned them. 'Might be dangerous stuff, especially when you aren't used to it.'

'We'll watch it,' Daniel promised.

'Back on my number by six,' Caroline added.

'Enjoy yourselves.'

'We expect to,' Daniel told him.

They set off through the sunny afternoon, and ended down by the river, where, in Embankment Gardens, they took two deck chairs and sat dreamily planning their future – consuming, at the same time, tea and ice cream. Afterwards, pleased with each other and the world in general, they sauntered back to St Anne's Square.

Outside Caroline's flat, they were brought out of their euphoric haze with a rude jerk, as they encountered Robert and Ginny. Caroline had overlooked the fact that they'd come up to spend the night, since they were to meet the Sneath-Robinsons for dinner at the Dorchester. They were on their way there now, looking up and down for a taxi.

'There you are, Caroline,' Robert exclaimed at once. 'I was afraid we were going to miss you.' He paused. 'Oh, and – er – Daniel. Yes.'

Ginny nudged him peremptorily.

Robert gulped. 'Haven't seen you,' he began, pulling himself together with a visible effort, 'since you and Caroline decided you were going to get married, have I? Best wishes,' he added grudgingly, surveying the son-in-law he didn't want, and plainly trying to make the best of a bad job. 'Hope you'll be happy, Caroline, my dear.' Somewhere in the recesses of his mind he grasped, faintly, that he might have been less than enthusiastic. 'Better come along to the Dorchester with us, and we'll drink to it, eh?'

This took everyone by surprise, and there was a blank silence before Daniel pulled himself together. 'Thank you, sir,' he said courteously, but almost as if he were addressing a minimum of twenty people at a board meeting. 'That's very civil of you.' He'd decided, he was reminding himself, that he had to come to terms with Caroline's father, and now was clearly the moment to begin. Without hesitation. 'Caro and I would appreciate it immensely if you felt inclined to drink to our future.'

Caroline gasped. They would? Was he accepting the invitation? She'd been prepared for him to break the record for the hundred yards sprint, as he'd done on the previous occasion Robert and Ginny had come to the flat.

'We have considerable confidence in it ourselves,' he was concluding, smiling the endearing lopsided grin that always melted Caroline.

Robert, who on that weekend two years earlier had glimpsed only the angry schoolboy, now had an opportunity to see the capable registrar, adept at managing Sister, his chief, Wily Walter, Uncle Tom Cobleigh and all, including a load of sick kids and their often impossible parents. One more impossible parent succumbed.

'I suppose we'd better go, then,' Robert said uninvitingly. 'As you're coming, Caroline, we could use the car – there don't seem to be any taxis about.'

So they drove to the Dorchester, drank champagne cocktails with the Sneath-Robinsons, and then extricated themselves, saying they had to return to the Central.

'Better ring across, I suppose,' Daniel said reluctantly, when they reached Caroline's flat. 'In case they've been trying to reach either of us – we didn't bargain for a session at the Dorchester. Adrian may be doing his nut by now. It's nearly seven.'

But Adrian said all was quiet, and nobody loved them.

'Good,' Daniel said, making a face at Caroline. 'We'll be here for the next couple of hours, and then at my place, if you want us.'

'Right.'

'At your place?' Caroline asked.

'When we've had that bacon and egg you promised me – more than two years since we had bacon and egg together, remember?'

'I remember.'

'After that, I thought we might adjourn. Then we won't be around when your father and Ginny return from the Sneath-Robinsons.'

'Good idea.'

What they neither of them suspected was that at that moment Sarah, lonely and tired and more than a little distraught, was roaming St Anne's Square.

The hospital in which she'd trusted had failed her.

At Waterloo she hadn't been able to see her father anywhere in the cafeteria. It had been a bitter blow. She'd been so certain he'd be there, waiting for her.

He was, in fact, sitting in the train still, just approaching Willesden – British Rail's bus had done the round of the stations on the line, and had taken nearly as long to reach Watford from Hemel Hempstead, less than ten miles as the crow flies, as Sarah had taken to come up from Stonebridge.

In his absence, Sarah, with almost the last of the housekeeping money, went to the counter and bought herself a ham sandwich and a glass of milk. It wasn't very good, but it would have to do. While she ate it, she'd be able to decide what she was going to do. In any case, Dad might arrive while she was eating.

With this in mind, she chose a table where she could watch the entrance, and made the sandwich last as long as possible. But he didn't come, and she began to wonder if he hadn't meant this cafeteria at all. Might there be another one in the station, and was he sitting there, waiting for her, wondering what had become of her? She'd go and look for him.

She soon discovered that there were a number of other places her father might have meant, but the trouble was, she couldn't find him in any of them. What was she going to do if she didn't meet him?

She would ring Sue. At Hemel Hempstead. That was it. She had only to say she had somehow missed Dad, and Sue would tell her what to do next.

She found a telephone box and rang the number. It rang on, unanswered. Sue had taken the baby and gone to spend the day with her sister, and there was no one in the house. Perhaps, though, Sarah thought hopefully, while she was on the telephone Dad had arrived. Perhaps he was sitting waiting for her there. She would go back and look.

She just missed him. While she was telephoning, he had arrived, and had looked for the two of them, Mrs Wakefield and Sarah, in the cafeteria where Sarah had eaten her sandwich – she had been right all along. That had been the place he meant. When he failed to find them he was irritated, but unsurprised. They'd missed the train, of course. Typical. He'd check the other cafeterias in the station, just in case they'd made a mistake, and then, if they weren't there, he'd telephone that warden fellow again, and be told, he was sure, that they had fiddled about and missed the bus, and would be on a later train. He'd have two hours to kill somewhere around this bloody station, crowded with returning holiday-makers with their cases and their kids.

Just as Sarah was wending her way back to the cafeteria after telephoning Sue, he set off briskly, missing her by thirty seconds.

Sarah had hardly expected him to be there, and sure enough, he wasn't. Just to be sure, though, about two minutes behind her father, she rechecked the other eating places in the station, and then, with a feeling of desperation, she went back to the telephone, to have another try at ringing Sue.

Her father was leaving the telephone kiosks as she approached. He was a worried man now. Mr Denman had told him that Sarah was alone. Any father would have been upset to learn that his small daughter was roaming unaccompanied about a London railway terminus, probably penniless, but Mr Wakefield was agonized. Sarah's insulin and her diet had to be balanced. She might already be on the edge of coma.

He went to the station-master's office.

Sarah, telephoning, again obtained no reply, but she stood there, letting the ringing tone continue, while she wondered what to do next. Her case seemed very heavy now, and the caravan she'd been so eager to quit a haven of security. Insidiously, panic began to rise within her, though she fought it back strenuously. And then the solution to her problems sprang into her mind. Dr Milne and Dr Harcourt had told her always to remember there was a hospital full of people to look after her, on Sundays just as much as any other day. So she would go to the Central and ask for Dr Milne. She would know exactly what to do.

Only thirty seconds before the loudspeakers began asking her to go to the station-master's office, where her father was waiting for her, she left the station on her way to the Central.

The first set-back she met was to find outpatients closed. This was the entrance she knew, and where she felt at home. Uncertainly, she tramped on, until she came to Casualty. If she'd gone in, she would have been looked after. But an ambulance was outside, unloading a stretcher, a white-coated doctor and two nurses were receiving it, there were machines and tubes going in all directions, and she was frightened off. Perhaps she should go to the ward. The trouble was, she was achingly tired by now, her case weighed a ton, and she felt more lost that she'd ever done in her life. She had no one. She'd somehow lost Dad, she couldn't get back to Stonebridge or on to Hemel Hempstead because she had no money left – the last of it had gone on her bus fare to the Central. What with misery, on top of exhaustion and lack of food, she was beginning to be muddled and far less competent at looking after herself. She tried to remember how to reach the ward from the street, but she couldn't find the right entrance. She'd lost her nerve by now, in any case. The day had been so long, and all the time she'd been bracing herself for action. She didn't feel able to face the main entrance, somehow her legs failed to carry her into this wide and intimidating foyer, and she walked slowly on past it, scuffing her feet and despising herself. She was being babyish. Perhaps, though, if she went on a bit further she'd find a door she knew, one that would lead her to the ward. Sister Heslip would be there, as it was Sunday, and though she could on occasion be sharp, she'd know what to do.

She came to a corner, and walked on round it. Here was a quiet entrance. Perhaps she should go in here and ask. In fact, she must go in. She couldn't go on putting off the moment any longer. She must be sensible, go in and ask for Dr Milne.

Bravely, she did this. But the receptionist shook her head. Sarah was enquiring in the Private Wing, where only the consultants' names were listed. 'Sorry, dear,' she said – she was a part-timer, who filled in on Sundays and for staff holidays only. 'No Dr Milne here. Ask at the main entrance, I should, if I were you.'

'Thank you very much,' Sarah said politely, and turned away, her confidence badly dented. She hadn't for a second imagined that if she once asked for Dr Milne there would be anyone in the hospital who wouldn't recognize her name. What was she going to do now? If there were people about who didn't even know her Dr Milne, how was she possibly going to make them understand what she needed? And she certainly couldn't expect anyone but Dr Milne, or perhaps Dr Harcourt, to set about finding her father or getting her to Hemel Hempstead. She'd had a secret hope that Dr Milne might have driven her there, but no one else was going to put her in a car and take her to Hemel Hempstead, that was for sure. So what was she going to do? It was getting late, and even Sister Heslip, that last resort, would probably have gone off duty.

In the morning outpatients would be open. She could go in there, and someone would be bound to find Dr Milne for her. But that was tomorrow. What was she to do tonight?

When she was little, Dad always said if ever she was lost, she was to go straight up to a policeman, and he would see she arrived home safe and sound. But that was for babies. She'd told them all she could look after herself, and she could, too. If only she could think what to do next. She ought to be able to think of something. It was a nuisance that she was so tired, and that this seemed to affect her being able to think. If only she could think about it properly, she'd be able to decide what to do. If she could just sit down and rest for a bit, she'd be better.

There was that square round the corner from the hospital, where she and Mum had a picnic when they came to outpatients. There were seats there. That was what she'd do. She'd go and sit in the square, and think it all out again from the beginning. If only she could find it. And her case, even though she kept changing it from one hand to the other, seemed so very heavy. The square, though, had been very near outpatients, only just round the corner, she was sure.

St Anne's Square, it said on the railings. She'd found it. She cheered up a little, though she knew finding the square wasn't really the end of her troubles. She ought to do what Dr Milne and Dr Harcourt had told her, even if it was difficult and nobody seemed to know. She ought to go to the main entrance and keep on asking for Dr Milne until somebody was found who did know her. That was what she ought to do. But she'd have a sit-down first, because she was most terribly tired, and she was beginning to feel she could hardly walk another step.

And then, just when she was feeling her worst, everything suddenly came right. She could hardly believe her eyes, but it was true. There in front of her, drawn up at the side of the square, was Dr Milne's familiar old Rover, that she'd always driven in Stonebridge, and that she and Dr Harcourt had come to fetch her in from Waterloo. Dr Milne's car. Like a home from home. Dr Milne must be somewhere about, too, in one of the houses. If only the car was unlocked, she could even sit in it and wait for her. She wouldn't mind.

She tried the doors, and at first she thought she was going to be unlucky, because both doors in the front were locked. But the back passenger door opened, and she climbed thankfully in. Sanctuary.

In the car it was warm and close. Relaxing. She calmed down, and began to feel sleepy, so she lay down on the back seat and stretched herself out comfortably, secure at last. There was surely something she ought to have done, though. With determination, she roused herself, and conscientiously, hazily, gave herself her evening insulin.

A fatal error. She'd had nothing to eat since her ham sandwich hours earlier, and her blood sugar was already shockingly low. Instead of saving her life, her insulin could kill her. Unaware, she drifted into sleep.

An hour later, Caroline and Daniel, after a supper of bacon and egg and coffee spent, like that faraway breakfast, holding hands and gazing entranced into one another's eyes, came out on their way to Daniel's flat, where they intended at last to spend a night of rapturous – and undisturbed – love. Engrossed in their own affairs, they sauntered along arm in arm, passing the Rover without a second glance, unconscious of anyone or anything but the joy of being together.

Halfway along the square Caroline stopped. A vague unease was nagging her. 'Did I lock the passenger doors?' she asked, abruptly cutting through their mutual absorption. 'When we got back from the Dorchester, I mean. Do you remember?'

He shook his head. 'No memory trace, I'm afraid. I was thinking of other things.'

'Me, too. That's just what makes me wonder. I'd better check – I still carry my emergency case there, you see. I don't usually forget to lock up, I know, but – '

'But we did have champagne cocktails. We'll go back and have a quick look, shall we?'

They returned to the car, and checked. All doors locked.

'False alarm,' Daniel said. 'But it was as well to be sure.'

'I didn't really think I could have forgotten, it's such a habit, but I must say I don't actually remember locking the passenger doors at the back.'

She was right. She hadn't. But Sarah, fiddling about and making herself comfortable, had, unaware, slipped the inside lock.

Daniel leant forward and peered in. 'I hope your bag isn't out on the seat in full view,' he remarked. 'That would be to invite trouble.' His voice altered. 'Caro,' he said. 'Young Sarah Wakefield's in there. Keys, stat.'

After that, everything happened at speed. Daniel drove round the corner to Casualty, where Caroline ran in with the small unconscious form limp in her arms, while he parked the car and then joined her in Casualty.

'She's a diabetic child – we've had her in the ward recently,' Caroline had told Dr Ingram, the night casualty officer. 'Shall I handle it, or would you prefer . . .'

'No, no, carry on,' he said. 'Your patient. Do we happen to know how long she's been like this?'

Caroline shook her head. 'We found her in the back of my car just now. She could have been there for, let's see – '

'From the time you parked when we got back from the Dorchester,' Daniel said. 'About seven.'

'Nearly nine now. Two hours, at the worst.'

'And it may be less. We must hope a good deal less.'

'You're wondering about brain damage?'

'Always a possibility, isn't it?'

They were working as they talked, and they'd already given the first injection of sterile glucose, were now setting up a drip.

'What's a diabetic child as young as this doing in London on her own at this hour, anyway?' Dr Ingram asked.

'I can't imagine.' Caroline was short. 'But her parents are divorced, and she was due to go to live with her father, on her mother's remarriage. She wrote to me about it. Perhaps she was on her way.'

'*Alone?*' The casualty officer was shocked.

'Wouldn't surprise me.' Caroline was bitter. Working on the inert little body, striving to retain its hold on life, any feeling of sympathy for Mrs Wakefield had left her.

By amazing luck, they'd got to Sarah in time to save her life, and glucose was flowing into her bloodstream. She wouldn't die. But what if that indomitable little personality had gone for ever? Caroline felt she could not bear it if that bright little spirit was to be extinguished, only a body living on, vegetable-like and moronic. Or the spirit might remain, but paralysis impair her activity, cripple her for the rest of her days.

'She'll do now,' she said finally. 'Don't you think? But we'll have to admit her.'

'Will you get on to the ward, or shall I?' Dr Ingram asked.

'Perhaps it would be better if I did,' Caroline suggested.

'Less argument,' he agreed, with a wry smile, and Caroline went to the telephone.

While she was arranging admission, the staff nurse found the Hemel Hempstead address and telephone number in Sarah's anorak pocket, and showed it to Dr Ingram. 'This may have been where she was making for,' she said. 'Anyway we could ring the number and see.'

Daniel came over and took a look. 'That's it,' he said. 'That's her father's address. She must have been on her way to him – poor little kid, she was so keen to go. I wonder what went wrong?'

Inside half an hour they found out. For an anxious Sue was waiting at home, and put them straight on to Sarah's father. He was still at Waterloo, with the railway police, who were searching for Sarah there – one of them drove him straight to the Central, and he came up to the ward where they'd taken Sarah. He was one of the most worried men Caroline had ever met.

'Is she going to be all right, Doctor?'

'She's not going to die, Mr Wakefield. Fortunately we found her in time. But – ' She hesitated. To burden this frantic little man, so amazingly like Sarah in appearance, with the worst of all possibilities, as soon as he appeared, seemed needlessly unkind. On the other hand, he had to be prepared.

'Got her room ready and everything,' he blurted out. During the long, anxious hours at Waterloo, this thought had been destroying him as surely as any other nightmare possibility. The thought that after all his carpentry and painting, all the loving care that had been poured into making ready Sarah's small bedroom in the new house, she might never occupy it. 'Every evening, I've worked on it,' he said. 'Made fitted cupboards for her, and a worktop between for a desk, see? Painted it all a nice yellow, and Sue papered the walls and made new curtains. Really nice it looks, my Sarah's room.' He seemed to be rambling on purposelessly, but he wasn't. 'Is she going to be able to come home with me, Doctor.' His eyes implored reassurance.

And she couldn't give it to him. 'I hope so.' She was sober. 'We just have to wait and see. There's no more we can do. It's a question, you see, of how long she was unconscious before we got to her. Whether' – she had to say it at last – 'whether her brain has been damaged at all.'

'Her brain damaged? My Sarah?' Mr Wakefield, who'd been given a chair by the bed, stared up at Caroline, and then hid his face. His shoulders shook. 'Oh God,' he muttered. 'My clever Sarah. My quick little darling. Her brain damaged? Oh God, no. No.'

Caroline held his quivering shoulder. About three times the size of Sarah's, yet it felt astonishingly the same, quaking and bony. The shoulder of someone needing comfort. 'We must keep on hoping. She may be quite all right. It's only a possibility. We'll have an idea when she comes to.'

When Sarah at last opened her eyes, Caroline was there, alongside her father. Her gaze crossed contentedly from one to the other, and she smiled beatifically. 'Dad,' she said. 'I knew my Dr Milne would find you.'

Caroline left them holding hands, and walked back down the ward.

Daniel appeared at her side. He'd been waiting for her. She smiled at him. Finding him beside her made her forget her exhaustion – and it was going to be like this for the rest of their lives.

She was too tired to speak – but she didn't need to. Holding hands, they walked out of the hospital and along the quiet, deserted square.